D1713514

Meant
To Be
Mine

CARA MAXWELL

Prologue

"Give it back to me Terry! Give it back!" The small girl wailed, jumping as high as she could in her attempts to reach the doll held aloft over her head by the taller boy. One of the desperate jumps resulted in a nasty landing on her knee, leading to a scrape and another round of bellowing tears.

"It's not nice to pick on little girls." A young but convincingly authoritative voice said from several yards away. The little girl pushed her mussed brown hair away from her eyes to see the owner approaching, a little boy equally tall to the one holding her doll hostage.

"Stay out of it," The bully sneered. The little girl did not see clearly what happened next from her vantage point on the ground where she held her scraped knee. But Terry squealed and ran away, while her doll was dropped onto the ground in front of her.

"Thank you," she said quietly as she scooped the doll into her lap. She sat cross-legged and looked down, somewhat embarrassed. But she couldn't resist asking: "Did you kick him?"

Her question was met with a small chuckle. "Yes, I did." The young boy answered. He crouched down on the ground next to her, but she still didn't look at him. "Are you alright?"

"I should have kicked him." She whispered, earning her another laugh from her savior. He kindly patted her on the shoulder.

"He would have trounced you, he's a big bully."

"Why didn't he trounce you?" Raising her eyes for the first time, she examined her rescuer. He was tall for his age, with short dark hair, close in color to hers. He looked like he might have been her brother, if she had a brother. Except for his eyes; his eyes were a stunning blue that made her wish for eyes just like his rather than her plain brown ones.

The older boy gave her a confident smile. "He wouldn't dare. I'm the lord of the land." He said in a gallant voice, flourishing his arms to indicate the surrounding landscape. She couldn't help giggling. His self-assured expression faltered a bit. "What's so funny?"

"We're on the wrong side of the stream. You're standing on *my* land." She pulled herself to her feet and smiled widely.

The boy looked around hesitantly. "Are you sure?"

She nodded assuredly. "Oh yes, Papa walks with me every day, and he tells me so. But he tells me it will all be mine one day." She said proudly, putting her hands on her hips.

"Surely not! How can my land come to you, when I know it will come to me?" He seemed even more confused. She shrugged nonchalantly, already beginning to lose interest in this conversation, as a young child does.

"I have to be going now. Mama says I must change my dress before we go to dinner. Thank you for saving me!" She smiled brightly, and then ran quickly in the opposite direction, clutching her beloved doll safely under her arm.

"You skipped a chapter," she said without opening her eyes.

"I certainly did not!" He protested. She was lying in the grass, enjoying the warm breeze. She may have drifted off for a few moments, but she was still certain he had skipped a chapter.

"How did he get off the boat then?" She questioned.

"If you know the book so well, why am I reading it?" He argued back.

"Because it is the gentlemanly thing to do, Theodore."

"Children, please do not raise your voices at one another." The voice of the governess floated across the air from a few yards away. Both children rolled their eyes.

Kelly sat up and looked around. Her governess was sitting primly on a blanket spread in the grass a few yards away, talking to the groom who had accompanied Theodore. Both Middleborough Manor and Willingham Park were too far away to see, but she could faintly hear the stream where Theodore had rescued her doll when she was five years old. "I was right, you know." She said, her eyebrows raised.

"Alright, so I did skip a chapter. But really, this is boring. Let's give the governess the slip and go do something fun." Theo suggested with a guilty grin.

"That's not what I was talking about," Kelly returned his smile. "When you rescued my doll from that wretched Terry, I said that eventually, this would all be mine."

"Ours," Theo corrected, trying to look superior. Kelly rolled her ten-year-old eyes again as he continued. "This will all be ours."

"Oh, I suppose there are worse people to share with than you." Kelly stuck her tongue out at Theo. Theo nudged her arm playfully before getting to his feet.

"Come on; let's find something better to do." He held out his hand to pull Kelly up. Shaking her head, fully aware that whatever he had in mind would certainly get them into trouble, Kelly put her hand into his.

"Calm down, Kelly, we will be there momentarily." Her mother said with annoyance.

"It's been months and months, Mama!" Kelly said excitedly, leaning as far out the window as she could as she tried to judge their distance from Willingham Park. They were nearing the bend in the drive, which meant it would be in sight momentarily. She could barely contain herself; it seemed like forever since Theo's father had sent him away to school, and Kelly had been hopelessly bored without him.

"And I'm sure young Theodore will behave very appropriately, as I expect you to. Kelly!" Her mother lectured, but her call was too late. The carriage had halted and thirteen-year-old Kelly had launched herself from it. She started to fly up the steps but stumbled to a hurried halt when she saw the people awaiting them.

Lord Alston, Theo's father, was tall and aloof. Even from a distance, it was clear that he was not the type to make idle conversation. His wife, Lady Alston, had light brown hair arranged in an elegant coiffure. She was the image of everything a countess should be, calm, composed, with a welcoming smile on her face as she waited to graciously welcome their guests. Of course, Kelly was most concerned about the third member of the party. Theo was his father in miniature; dark hair, tall even as a teenager. Kelly could barely contain her eagerness as she slowed and tried to climb the last few stairs daintily, as her mother was always imploring her to do.

"Good evening, Miss Collins," Lord Alston said formally. Kelly bobbed a hasty curtsy to Lord and Lady Alston before turning excitedly to their third companion. "Theo! I've got so much to tell you!"

"Good evening, Miss Collins," Theo repeated formally. He bowed slightly. Kelly took a step back in confusion. That was quite unlike Theo. She watched him carefully, expecting his characteristic grin to creep across his face at any moment, his laugh to tell her that he was joking with her. But his face and demeanor stayed calm and cool.

"Good evening Lord Alston, Lady Alston." Kelly's mother came gracefully up the steps behind her. "My goodness, Theodore, how grown-up you look!" She exclaimed, curtseying and holding out her hand formally. Theo took it, kissing her hand and bowing. Then she turned to his parents and followed them inside. Kelly remained frozen in front of Theo. What was wrong? Why was he being so...strange?

"Shall we go in?" Theo said awkwardly after a few moments, holding out his arm.

"I....well....yes..." Kelly trailed off. She didn't know what to do or to say. So she picked up the formality her mother had trained her for, the formality which she had never once experienced or expected with Theo. She put her arm in his and allowed him to lead her inside.

Chapter 1

*S*he supposed there were worse things; like going to a penal colony in Australia or being kidnapped by pirates in the Caribbean. It must be worse to spend the day in the stocks or to go days without food or water. As she sat in the carriage bouncing along towards London, Kelly Collins continued to make a list in her head of things that were worse than being shipped off to London unceremoniously by her parents with one express mission: find your fiancé and convince him to marry you.

"Sit up straight, Kelly, you'll never catch anyone's eye if you slouch like that." Her mother's voice cut sharply into her mental list-making.

Kelly gritted her teeth as she straightened her back against the uncomfortable carriage seat, but she did not respond. Her mother's words had the unavoidable result of making her think about her current predicament. Stifling a defeated sigh, she returned to her list: being branded with a cattle iron, getting run over by a carriage…

"The Countess of Crawford is giving a ball tonight. I have it on good authority that Lord Alston will be there, so that is where we will put in our first appearance." Claire Collins interrupted again. She was fidgeting nervously, turning a handkerchief over again and again in her clenched hands. Kelly forced herself to take a few breaths before responding. She knew her mother wasn't trying to make things worse. She was trying to formulate a plan, a plan to bring Kelly's wayward fiancé to heel. And from the looks of it, her mother was just as uncomfortable and apprehensive about the whole endeavor as she was.

Her mother seemed to have aged a decade in the past few years. Her brown hair was streaked with gray and had lost the bright coppery sheen that Kelly herself had inherited. Claire's deep brown eyes, also the mirror of her daughters, were fanned with lines of worry.

Kelly did not know the exact details; her parents had tried to spare her from the worst of it. But she had gleaned from half-overheard conversations, offhand comments, and a little snooping that they had made some investments which had turned out badly. The result was that their estate, her beloved home at Middleborough Manor, was deeply in debt. The Collins family was in near danger of losing the home their family had inhabited for three centuries, and having to let go the dozens of workers who depended on the estate for their livelihood.

Kelly sighed, reached over, and took her mother's hands firmly in her own. "Mama, it will be alright. We will find him, and I will sit up straight, and he will be dazzled by me." She straightened her back exaggeratedly, pointing her nose high in the air. Her attempt at levity earned a small smile from her mother.

However, her smile quickly faded into a concerned frown. "You understand how important this is, Kelly? Lord Alston must be made to honor the arrangement…"

Kelly held up her hand to cut her mother off.

"I completely understand. It's not as if we are up to anything untoward. We are merely fulfilling a longstanding contract." Kelly recited blandly.

"A legally binding contract!" Claire added in elevated tones, clearly unconvinced of her daughter's understanding of the gravitas of the situation.

"Legally binding to us, Mama, but perhaps that is not how he sees it. These things are easily shaken off these days." The instant Kelly said it, she wished she hadn't. Her mother's face turned sheet white. She squeezed her mother's hand in what she hoped was a reassuring manner, while inwardly scolding herself. Kelly knew the stakes and her mother's predisposition to excessive worry. She tried to sound convincing as she reassured her mother. "He will honor the betrothal. His father made it in good conscience, and after all these years, he cannot possibly mean to shirk his responsibility."

Kelly saw the calming effect her words had on her mother, but she was not at all convinced by them herself. Wasn't the whole reason they were on their way to London because he was not honoring the betrothal? Because her 18th birthday had come and gone, and then her 19th, and then her 20th, with no contact from her supposed fiancé? Kelly sighed again,

resigned.   She had no choice in the matter; her
family's estate was crumbling, and without the
finances this union would bring, it would quickly
disappear out from under them.

Growing up, she had always taken her betrothal to
Theo as a given. From her earliest memory, they had
both known that eventually, they would marry. And
as far as she could tell, they had both been completely
accepting of that fact. She tried to think back on any
sign in their adolescence that would have pointed to
Theodore's distaste for the arrangement, but she
couldn't land on anything.

Kelly and Theo had grown up together; they had
studied and read, played, and gotten into mischief.
When Kelly was thirteen, Theodore had gone away
to boarding school. After that, he was a completely
different person. He didn't smile or tease the way he
always had. He became rigidly formal with her, with
everyone for that matter. But they had still seen each
other during holidays from school, had shared many
meals and many polite conversations. They had
acknowledged their parents' plans for their union
without protest. What was giving him pause now that
the time was at hand? Kelly hadn't the faintest idea.

She closed her eyes and leaned her head against the
side of the carriage. Perhaps sleep would be a reprieve
until they arrived in London and she had to face
reality.   Instead, she dreamt of summer days spent
playing outside, of a knight in shining armor rescuing
her from bullies and family tragedy alike, and of
bright blue eyes.

"Lord   Alston,   Earl   of   Willingham."   His
announcement into the ballroom garnered several

turned heads. He cut a dashing figure dressed in all black, as was his usual custom. Certainly, there were several young ladies, and several older ones, whose hearts skipped with excitement as they admired the young earl. But once they quickly looked him over and decided he didn't merit immediate scandal, the crowd moved on to other pursuits. Theodore ignored all of their attentions and made straight for the far corner, where he saw his friend Henry Warsham talking to several other male acquaintances.

"Where have you been hiding, Theo?" Henry clapped him on the shoulder and passed him a drink. "I thought for sure some lady had finally sunk her claws into you!"

Theo's allowed his mouth to curl into a lazy smile. "Well, I wouldn't call her a lady, but she certainly was entertaining." He said coolly. This earned him a round of laughs from the men assembled. Henry smiled knowingly and steered his friend away from the group a bit, under the guise of getting another drink. His offhand remark, and Theo's contrived response, were played out exactly the way the *ton* expected them to be. They did not, however, reveal anything below the surface about the mysterious and reserved Theodore, Earl of Willingham. Of course, Henry knew him better than that. They had been friends since their boarding school days.

"Where have you been off to, Theo? You disappeared for nigh a month! Maddie's been after me to have you 'round for dinner, but I hadn't the courage to tell her I had no idea where you were." Henry said when they were alone.

"Oh, just here and there," Theo answered nonchalantly. He refilled his drink at one of the many punchbowls and took a sip. Henry didn't press for a further answer; if his friend wanted to share, he would in due course. Over more than a decade of friendship, Theo and Henry had developed a comfortable rhythm.

Theo wasn't generally a forthcoming person. It wasn't that he was rude or secretive, he just preferred not to discuss himself or his personal life. It had been drilled into him from the moment he became a man; the face you presented to the world should be well crafted and controlled, no matter what storms brewed beneath the surface. If there was anything his father had taught him, it was that.

"Well, now that you're back you will have to come to dinner. Once Maddie sees you there will be no escape." As if her ears were burning, Henry's wife appeared from amid the ever-growing crowd of revelers. Her distinctive laugh could be heard above the din of the crowd, and even in the busy throng, she stood out. She wasn't a tall woman, but her boisterous demeanor always seemed to command attention.

"Theo! You're here!" She smiled widely, offering him her hand and grinning as he kissed it dutifully. "You're a beast, to disappear like that for weeks without explanation!" She chided only half-jokingly as she brushed her long blonde hair back over her shoulder. She suspected that he had been avoiding her attempts to set him up with a female acquaintance of hers, but she couldn't be sure.

"If I think you're cross with me, I will be truly wounded," He said back, without the slightest circumspection. Madison laughed indulgently. She had a soft spot for Theo; she had ever since her husband had introduced her to him. He always seemed so alone and so damnably comfortable with that fact that it was her dearest endeavor to make sure the opposite was true. Therefore, she always including him in gatherings and trying to find him a good woman.

"You know I can never be cross with you, Theo. But how am I supposed to throw eligible lady after eligible lady into your path if you won't stick around?" She said brazenly, crossing her arms.

"Has the thought occurred to you that I'm not interested in an eligible lady?" He answered truthfully, arching his eyebrows. He wasn't a fool; he knew what Madison had been up to for ages, despite how he might feign ignorance. And he wasn't about to get himself saddled with one of the silly women she kept trying to entangle him with.

Madison raised hers in challenge. "Not interested? Hmm, we will see. In any matter, I shall expect you for dinner tomorrow night. You can tell us all about what you have been up to." She said pointedly.

"That's not likely," Henry put in, giving Theo a conspiring grin.

"But he'll accept," Madison said confidently. Theo nodded his acquiesce, but his attention was on the other side of the ballroom, on the woman who had just entered.

She was wearing a light shade of brown that was unusual for a young woman but complimented her rich dark brown hair; beautiful dark hair that was partially pinned up, but already trying to escape the pins. Even from a distance, he could appreciate her generously rounded breasts and hips. Though he was certain she was single; the way she moved, glancing back at her companion as if for approval, suggested she was chaperoned and therefore unmarried. She wasn't his usual type, he usually preferred his women a bit older and more experienced. There was no guessing about what they wanted from him.

But the newcomer caught his attention and held it. He couldn't see her well so far across the ballroom, but there was something vaguely familiar about her. He wasn't able to place her exactly, but the way she absently tossed an errant curl over her shoulder and tilted her head to speak to her companion rang with recognition. Theo vaguely noted the other woman with her; her hair was lighter, and from the way she dressed he guessed she was older, though he could not tell for sure because she was turned away from him.

The older woman leaned over and whispered to the liveried man standing at the doorway so he could announce their presence to the assembled crowd. Theo turned his head so he could clearly hear as the servant announced: "Lady Claire Collins, Baroness of Middleborough, and her daughter, Miss Kelly Collins."

Chapter 2

Kelly surveyed the wide array of people as she descended the stairs into the main ballroom. Her mother led the way a few steps ahead of her, clearly charting a path for her to follow. Kelly was grateful. She had not attended an event this large since her come-out two years ago. Her parents could not afford a long and expensive season, so after her presentation and a few social events, they had returned to the country. As it was, she had no idea how they were affording this excursion into the capital. The thought reminded her all too unkindly of her mission.

By the time Kelly had descended the stairs into the crush of the ballroom, her mother was already engaged in conversation with an older woman who Kelly vaguely recognized as Countess Crawford, their hostess. "I am so happy to see you back in town!" She exclaimed to Claire Collins.

"Yes, we thought it would be important to bring Kelly." Her mother answered. To Kelly, the comment seemed laced with implication, begging the Countess to ask the pertinent follow-up question.

"But of course! It's time for this young lady to catch a husband!" Kelly winced at the Countess's forwardness, but her mother seemed unfazed. This was exactly the line of conversation that she had wanted to bring up. Her mother certainly wasn't wasting any time in moving forward with her plans to bring Theodore on board.

"Actually, Kelly is already betrothed. A longstanding agreement made by fathers long ago," she trailed off. This time Kelly was sure it was deliberate. For all of her doubt on the carriage ride to town, Claire certainly seemed to have a plan of attack.

"Oh! Who indeed?" the Countess asked with interest. She was clearly thrilled that she would be the starting point for a new piece of *ton* gossip.

"To Lord Alston, Earl of Willingham. Willingham and Middleborough are neighboring estates, as you might know. As I said, the arrangement has been in place since they were both quite young." Kelly's mother said without missing a beat. Kelly let out a breath she didn't know she was holding. There it was; the cat was out of the bag for all of society to see. Now either her fiancé would feel pressured to honor the betrothal, or she would be humiliated in front of the *ton*.

"Lord Alston is here! He was announced not five minutes before you!" The Countess said excitedly. She began scanning the room, trying to locate the specific guest. Her eyes searched the ballroom, dance floor, and outskirts already quite crowded with guests. Unsuccessful, she turned a markedly disappointed gaze back to Kelly and her mother. "Well, he is about somewhere. I'm sure you will enjoy catching up with him."

"Indeed," Kelly nodded politely as the Countess moved away to greet another guest. For the next hour, Kelly allowed herself to be pulled around behind her mother as she renewed acquaintances, but she stood somewhat back from the exchanges. She felt many people's eyes on her. Could her mother's declaration have spread that quickly? Or was there something wrong with her appearance?

Kelly had never been comfortable in London, amidst the *haute ton*. The women here were so elegant, graceful, and well-spoken. Not necessarily intelligent, Kelly thought with a small smile, and often quite superficial. When she had been in London for her debut, she had been surprised by how the women of the *ton* gossiped so negatively about others and kept themselves interested in such vain pursuits. But they didn't stumble over their words, as Kelly often did when she was nervous. And they certainly considered her somewhat inferior, given her rural upbringing.

But Kelly was fine with that. She preferred the quieter pace of life back at Middleborough – the fresh air, the rolling hills, the lack of intrigue and gossip. But she had come to London to save that very life, she reminded herself. Her home, and all the beloved people that inhabited it, were worth whatever uneasiness she might feel now.

"Excuse me; I'm going to get a bit of fresh air." She said to her mother and her companions after a while. She was feeling stifled by the density of people and the weight of her mission. She needed a few moments alone.

Retreating into the cool night air on the terrace, Kelly was thankful to find it relatively deserted. The cold tinge in the air had discouraged all but a few scattered people from venturing outside. Rubbing her hands up and down her bare arms to generate heat, she walked slowly along the railing and gazed absently over the darkened gardens.

"Good evening, Miss Collins."

A deep voice broke her reverie suddenly. Spinning around to find the source, Kelly instantly took a step back when she did.

"I...what..." She opened her mouth to speak, but the words seemed to die on her tongue. This earned a dark chuckle from her companion.

"You still have a way with words, I see," Theo said dryly.

Kelly frowned. "Theo," she managed to say quietly, curtseying slightly but keeping her eyes on him. She looked him over carefully, examining how his shoulders had widened and he had grown even taller. Then she arrived at his eyes. His startlingly blue eyes had not changed at all. Theo always had a way of looking at her that made her feel like he could see right into her soul, past whatever words she was saying to the root of her feelings. Caught now in his gaze, she desperately hoped that wasn't still true.

She stared at him for a full minute before reality hit her in the stomach and she realized this was probably not the way to go about wooing him. Taking a deep breath, she forced a smile onto her face. "Good evening, Lord Alston. It is a pleasure to see you."

He considered for a moment before responding. "Indeed, a strange but not unpleasant coincidence." He nodded, his eyes narrowing as he looked at her more closely. The sunny girl had blossomed into a good-looking young woman. Her brown hair shined copper where it caught the light, and the tendrils that sprang loose accentuated her slim neck, which gave way to an ample bosom. Despite his years of acquaintance with the child, Theo felt a very real physical response to the woman standing before him. Taking firm control of himself, Theo asked: "What brings you and your mother to London, Miss Collins? As I recall, neither of you ever had much taste for it."

Kelly swallowed nervously. Despite the fact that they had not seen each other in five years, she immediately felt that he could read her too easily, knew her too well. He would see her deception instantly. "Why does any young woman come to town?" She said evasively, though her voice did not sound convincing.

"To find a husband. Are you husband-hunting, Miss Collins?" He raised an eyebrow, and Kelly got the feeling he was making fun of her. When was the last time Theo had teased her? She wondered to herself.

"Certainly nothing as crude as that," Kelly said defensively. Her brow furrowed unconsciously as she tried to form her next statement. "I…well, you and I…" but before she could get it out, they were interrupted.

"There you are, Lord Alston! I've been looking for you all evening!" Countess Crawford swept onto the terrace. Her declaration gained the attention of several guests standing near the doorway, who began eagerly listening in to the exchange. Before she could escape, Kelly saw Countess Crawford's eyes latch onto her as well. "Ah, and Miss Collins, I see you found your dear Lord Alston after all! Now, Theodore, I must admit I was quite surprised when Lady Collins told me that you and Miss Collins were betrothed! You've kept quite the secret all these years." She smiled widely, putting her hand familiarly on Theo's arm, the other on Kelly's.

Kelly looked up quickly to see how Theo would respond, but his face was inscrutable. The humor she had seen a few moments before was gone, and in its place was an aloof, unreadable mask. He looked right past Kelly as he answered calmly: "Our fathers made the contract many years ago." That was it. That was all he said, he neither confirmed nor denied the status of their relationship. Kelly felt herself slowly releasing the breath she didn't know she had been holding.

Countess Crawford seemed disappointed with this answer, frowning slightly. "So, when shall the happy occasion take place?" She prompted.

Again, Theo answered without emotion: "No concrete plans have been set as of yet." He said smoothly, in a tone that invited no further questions. Countess Crawford was unsatisfied, but she nodded and retracted her hand from Theo's arm, clearly feeling the chill of his demeanor.

"Well, I shall let you two continue your conversation; I've many people to see, after all…" She trailed off as she walked away, shooting a curious glance back at them over her shoulder as she retreated.

Theo turned to Kelly immediately. His face was not calm now; he looked like a veritable dragon ready to breathe fire. "I did not know our betrothal was common knowledge among the *ton*." He said harshly.

"I…I didn't…" Kelly stammered. But Theo did not seem interested in hearing her response. He turned on his heel and without further word, walked away.

Chapter 3

*H*er first thought upon waking was that she was already an utter failure. Kelly had been in London for less than 24 hours, and instead of impressing her wayward fiancé, she had managed to make him angry enough to storm out of a party in front of half of the London *ton*. She contemplated getting up, but thought better of it and lay back in bed.

This was not good, she thought to herself.

The stakes couldn't be higher for Kelly. Marriage to Theo meant Middleborough would be safe; the rolling hill and lush green forests would continue to be tended with love and care. The staff who had been with her family for as long as she could remember would maintain their positions. And her beloved parents, who had only ever tried to do their best for her, would have their pride and position rescued. She had no other option but to make this work.

As she closed her eyes, she tried to remember all the things she knew about Theodore Alston. From the moment he rescued her toy from the village bully, she had adored him. They found out about their relationship to one another, affianced as they were, not long after, but as children that hadn't fazed them a bit. They were fast friends; they grew up together. That was until Theo was sent away to boarding school. Nothing was ever the same after that. They still saw one another on holidays, but more to please their parents than because they had anything in common. It was as if the carefree and lovable boy she had known for so many years had disappeared overnight. There were no more lessons in tree climbing or adventures to be had after escaping the watchful eyes of adults. To this day, she had no idea what had changed so suddenly between them. She frowned at the thought. Maybe this was a mystery that would be unlocked now that she and Theodore were both adults. Maybe it was somehow related to his hesitation in marrying her.

She thought of the last time she had seen Theo, before the previous night of course. It had been at his father's funeral at Willingham Park. Theo had just finished school. Kelly was still only 15 so there was no expectation that they would marry immediately, but their parents had continued to arrange visits between them up until that point to maintain their acquaintance with one another. Not that it mattered; Theo was always so formal and guarded that Kelly felt she could have seen him every day and not known him any better. Was he still like that? She wondered. She thought she had experienced some humor last night before his mood turned sour. That was certainly a side she hadn't seen of him since he was trying to trick her into some sort of teenage shenanigans. But he had been cool and aloof when discussing their betrothal with Countess Crawford. He hadn't appeared ruffled at all until they were again alone and he had stormed off.

His father's funeral had been a large affair; for someone so highly ranked in the peerage, nothing less was expected. Theo's mother had presided over the event with quiet dignity, her silent son at her side. Kelly particularly remembered the luncheon at Willingham following the church service. Her mother had encouraged her to approach Theo and offer her personal condolences, as seemed appropriate for a man's future wife to do.

"I…I'm…your…very sorry…" She had been so nervous that she had stumbled over her words. Theo hadn't laughed at her then, as he had last night. He had just stared at her blankly. She vividly remembered the impulse she had in the moment, to reach over and take his hand in hers. She remembered acting on the impulse, feeling the warmth of his hand, seeing the surprise in his eyes at her action.

Then he gently squeezed her hand and quietly said "Thank you." He released her hand and moved past her to talk to another guest. That was it. He had spoken only two words to her, met her eyes for only a moment, and yet Kelly could still remember how sad and lonely those icy blue eyes had looked, in contrast to how warm and alive his hand had felt in hers. She sighed at the memory, not sure if she should count it among the happy ones or not.

Resigned to get up and face the day, she pulled herself out of bed and rang for her maid. She wasn't a fussy person and was dressed for the day quickly.

When she entered the dining room below, she found it empty. Mama must still be abed, she thought to herself as she sat down to eat.

"My lady, I'm so sorry to interrupt you," a footman poked his head in the door. "But your mother left this note for you." He held out a neatly folded piece of paper. Kelly frowned; she hadn't thought she had slept late, but her mother still seemed to have beaten her out of the gate.

"Thank you," She said absently, unfolding the note and reading. Well, it appeared her mother was wasting no time in renewing the acquaintances that would assure them entrance to all of the *ton's* social gatherings. Kelly was told to be ready that evening and to keep out of trouble for the day. Kelly felt a bit offended by that; what trouble could she possibly get into? She knew the stakes of this trip; she wouldn't get up to something foolish. She sighed and glanced out the window. The weather looked nice enough. Maybe she would just take a book and go read in the park.

"You disappeared quickly last night," Henry said as he slowed his horse to a walk alongside Theo's.

"The company had a sobering effect," Theo said ominously. Henry was unfazed. Theo sighed inwardly. He did not want to discuss the previous night's events. Encountering Kelly Collins had been like being hit over the head with a club. It had always been like that with Kelly. She was too attractive for her own good and too intelligent for his. Though he did find the fact that she had not outgrown her mumbling worthy of a chuckle.

She had always been a good-looking child, but she had grown into a beautiful woman. The freckles on her cheeks had faded, and her body had filled in too many womanly curves for him to be comfortable with. Those eyes, he sighed inwardly, he had always been so easily swayed by them. From the time she was a giddy five-year-old begging him not to tell on her for stealing pastries from the kitchen, those eyes had been problematic for him. The fact that they were now accompanied by a lush body made him uneasy.

"I thought you liked the lady. You sure couldn't take your eyes off of her from the moment she walked in." Henry prodded, grinning at his friend. Theo's frown deepened.

"Sometimes things are not what they appear." He answered.

"Oh, stop being so cryptic." Henry rolled his eyes. "What was wrong with the girl?"

"It's a long story," Theo sighed.

"It's a big park," his friend countered.

"You never could leave well enough alone, could you Warsham?"

"Never," He answered with a grin. Theo rolled his eyes. Where did he even begin to explain his situation with Miss Collins? He might as well tell Henry. Now that Kelly was in London their involvement was going to become common knowledge soon. Hell, now that Countess Crawford knew it was only a matter of days before this juicy new gossip made the rounds.

"It's complicated," He began.

"Yes, I think we've established that." Henry teased.

"Enough, I'm not going into…"

"Alright, alright, I'll stop teasing. Do continue." Attempting a straight face and failing, Henry fiddled with his reins to stop from laughing outright at his friend's obvious discomfort.

Theo gave him a dark look but continued anyway. "I am already acquainted with Miss Collins, or at least I was in the past. Her father is the Baron of Middleborough, which adjoins Willingham."

"Please don't tell me this is a tail of spoilt virtue…"

"It's not," Theo said shortly. "Historically, the Barons of Middleborough and the Earls of Willingham have squabbled over the border between the two estates. One generation the line is drawn one place, then the next generation it changes a bit and both sides claim they have somehow been cheated by the other. My father had a wider vision than that; instead of arguing over a few acres here or there, he envisioned both estates incorporated into one. So, when we were both very young, Miss Collins' and I's fathers reached an agreement intended to unite our two estates and put to rest any dispute once and for all. In short, for most of our lives, Miss Collins and I have been…"

"Betrothed!" Henry finished with a whoop. He couldn't contain his laughter. Theo looked less than amused.

"I'm so glad you find this situation amusing, Warsham. Because she is now almost certainly come to London to stake her claim, such as it is."

"I'm surprised you haven't staked yours! There's the whole of Middleborough to be had. No wonder your father had you betrothed." He said sarcastically.

"I don't care about what my father wanted," Theo said shortly. "Nor am I bound by his land-thirsty obligations."

"So, you mean to toss her over, then?" Henry pulled up his horse rather abruptly, frowning at Theo. He knew Theo wasn't keen on the idea of marriage, especially one that was arranged by his father. But somehow, he couldn't picture him humiliating a lady in the way that Miss Collins would undoubtedly be if he publicly denounced their engagement.

Theo shrugged. He honestly wasn't sure what he was going to do about Miss Collins. For the time being, however, he was going to put this messy business from his mind. "Let's ride," he said as he kicked his mount into a canter. Henry sighed. This was surely going to be a messy business, he thought to himself before riding off after his friend.

Chapter 4

"May I share your bench?"

Kelly was startled from reading. "I beg your pardon?" She said automatically.

"May I share your bench?" The other woman repeated.

"Of course," Kelly responded. Gathering her wits about her, Kelly looked at the other woman. She was about the same age as her, perhaps a year or two older. Her long blonde hair was in a sleek braid that fell over one shoulder, and she was elegantly adorned in a lavender day dress. However, the way she threw herself down on the bench was anything but elegant. She proceeded to lean over her feet and started fiddling with her shoes, which were similarly elegant gray leather boots that reached just above her ankles. With a quick glance around the immediate vicinity to check for observers, she eased off one shoe and then the other, letting out a sigh of pleasure as she did so. Looking up, she saw Kelly's confused face.

She motioned to the shoes she had just removed. "My sister tells me these are the height of fashion in Paris, where she sent them from. Quite lovely, aren't they?" She grinned wryly, holding up the boot for examination. "The leather is very supple, and the buttons are quite ornate. Ivory, I believe" She said, before tossing the shoe down on the ground forcefully. "They are quite honestly the most uncomfortable things I have ever had the misfortune of owning."

Kelly couldn't stop the laugh that bubbled out of her. She instantly clapped her fist to her mouth to silence it, but the other woman was unperturbed. "Please, go ahead and laugh. I would laugh if my feet didn't ache so much." Leaning back, she closed her eyes and wiggled her recently liberated toes. "I really do think my sister is having a joke at my expense."

"I…" Kelly started to speak, but afraid that her words would muddle themselves as they usually did in situations where she was nervous, she bit her lip.

Her companion didn't seem to notice. "I feel I should introduce myself, as you've already seen more of my anatomy than my husband did before we were married. I am Madison Warsham."

"A pleasure to meet you, Lady Warsham. I am Miss Kelly Collins, of Middleborough." Kelly managed to say.

"Well Kelly, and I will call you that, as we are already so advanced in our acquaintance thanks to my sister's fashion advice, you are my savior." She said exaggeratedly, a quick smile coming to her face and instantly enhancing her beauty. "If I hadn't seen this bench, I probably would have sat right down in the grass."

Kelly laughed again. She quickly felt her tension and nervousness easing. "Right in the grass, my lady?"

"Maddie, you must call me Maddie. It wouldn't do for me to call you Kelly and you to waste time with all this 'my lady' business. We're to be friends, remember?" Madison's smiled widened. "And yes, I would have put myself right down in the grass and waited for my husband to come find me. He is riding around here somewhere." She cast a quick eye around them but did not spot him. Her eyes fell on Kelly's book. "What are you reading?"

"Oh, it's nothing special," Kelly said, showing Madison the book. "Just something to pass the time and keep me out of trouble, as my mother would say."

"Keep you out of trouble? Whatever kind of trouble would you get into?" Madison looked at the book for a second and then handed it back to Kelly with a quizzical look.

"I haven't the faintest idea." Kelly rolled her eyes. "But my mother is convinced I will make a muddle of this trip to London one way or another."

"Well, that's not the right outlook!" Madison said with a humph. But then a new thought twinkled in her eyes. "You're new to London then?"

"I haven't been here since my come-out when I was seventeen."

"And what brings you now?" Madison asked eagerly.

Kelly paused. "It's…complicated." She said slowly.

Madison's eyebrows raised, her interest piqued. "That sounds interesting," she said with an encouraging smile.

As much as she liked her new friend, Kelly wasn't quite ready to spill her secret yet. She didn't even really know who Madison was; a lady of standing, clearly, but who exactly was not clear. "It's not interesting. Just a mother worried about the usual things."

"Marriage, of course," Madison said bluntly. She could tell by the look on Kelly's face that she had guessed correctly. "That is all mothers of women our age worry about. Before I married Henry, my mother was an absolute lunatic, foisting me on every marriageable gentleman within the county lines."

"Well, at least it's not just me then," Kelly said with a sigh.

"But you're a pretty girl," Madison leaned back a bit, as if to get a better look at the picture that Kelly presented. "I can't imagine you haven't had offers." She observed frankly.

"Well, I haven't, exactly... as I said, it is complicated..." She trailed off. "This is a very unusual conversation," Kelly said, starting to feel uncomfortable.

Madison just laughed. "I suppose it is. We've only just met, but I feel instantly at ease with you. Perhaps because we have shared the traumatic experience of these shoes," she laughed again. "I've just the thing! To show your mother you can handle yourself perfectly well, I shall invite you to dinner tonight. Nothing formal, I assure you," Madison put up her hand when Kelly instantly started to protest. "Just my husband and a couple of friends. But it will show that you've gained the approval of an important societal matron, the Marchioness of Clydon." Madison straightened her back like a rod and put her nose up in the air in fake pomposity. Kelly couldn't help but laugh.

"Well, I don't think my mother will be able to argue with that," Kelly agreed. "But just how do you intend on getting home? You're not planning on walking through Piccadilly barefoot, are you? I can go fetch you some shoes to borrow and bring them back if you wait here."

"That is very sweet, but Henry should be along soon. He and Theo always ride back this way in the mornings. He'll lecture my ear off for walking out here alone, but then he'll be helpful enough…"

But Kelly did not hear what else Madison had to say. She had frozen when the name passed Madison's lips, as she sighted two riders turning down the lane and heading distinctly in their direction.

Chapter 5

"**H**enry!" Madison called, waving her hand in the air to catch the two men's attention. Kelly's first instinct was to wish that the ground would somehow swallow her up. She could tell the exact moment that Theo realized who she was, and the look of surprise followed by a deep frown made her want to sink into the bench itself. Madison appeared completely unaware of her distress. She was smiling broadly at the men as they closed the remaining yards between them.

Kelly forced herself to take a deep breath and sit up straight. She could not be a coward now. Too much was riding on her ability to charm the elusive Lord Alston into honoring their marriage contract. She had to be serene, attractive, interesting. The opposite of how she had behaved the previous night, she thought to herself ruefully. Trying her best to keep her nerves at bay, she fixed a sunny smile on her face.

"Oh Henry, it's about time you came along. We've been waiting for you!" Madison said with joking reprove. "I wore those awful shoes my sister sent me, and they've torn my feet to bits. I'm going to need to ride home with you." She said, gesturing down at the offending shoes with a crinkle of her eyebrows.

"Madison, have you taken your shoes off right here on the park bench?" Henry answered, shaking his head. "You wonder why people are always gossiping about you."

Madison pursed her lips in annoyance. "Yes, I have. And there is nothing scandalous about it. The only person who witnessed my ordeal was Miss Collins," she indicated Kelly, "And I assure you, her and I are already the dearest of friends."

Henry didn't respond immediately but looked quickly over at Theo, who was silent and looking at the ground. A smile slowly spread over his handsome face. "Miss Collins, it is a pleasure to meet you."

"Oh yes, Kelly, this is my husband Henry Warsham, Marquess of Clydon. Darling, this is Miss Kelly Collins." Madison said quickly. "And this handsome brute is Theodore Alston, Earl of Willingham."

"We are already acquainted," Kelly broke in, her smile steady. For a moment she was surprised by her own forwardness, but she decided to surge ahead. "It's a pleasure to see you again so soon, Lord Alston."

Theo wasn't looking at the ground anymore, but right at Kelly. Kelly was startled by the intensity of his gaze. She felt like he could see right through her sunny facade.

Theo's assessment of Kelly was much as it had been the night before; he just didn't know what to make of her. She couldn't have orchestrated this meeting as she had no way of knowing he would be in the park, nor arranged her chance meeting with Madison. Besides, the Kelly he had always known hadn't had a manipulative or calculating bone in her body.

Yet somehow, here they were face to face with one another again. He knew full well why she had come to London; it did not take a genius to puzzle it out. He hadn't ignored her father's many letters over the years out of spite or malice, he simply hadn't known how to nor wanted to deal with the situation. After three years, her family was ready to force the issue one way or the other. He didn't want to humiliate little Kelly Collins, but he also wasn't about to submit to the tortuous state of matrimony.

He had to convince Kelly that he was not a desirable husband. It was the truth, of course. He would never consent to make himself miserable for the rest of his life just for the sake of another person. And he knew the state of marriage was nothing short of miserable. He would convince her that he was not the one for her. She could break off the betrothal; that way she was blameless and he looked like the jilted one, a ding to his reputation that he could easily endure. Then she would find another husband, and he would be free to continue his life in peace. That was the game, and he was sure to be the winner.

He smiled at Kelly, noting the surprise that flitted across her face. "It's a pleasure to see you as well, Miss Collins."

Knowing she would stumble if she spoke, Kelly nodded. This was certainly a different Theodore than the evening before. Now he was being cordial; what was he playing at? Thankfully, Madison jumped in and saved her from having to come up with something appropriate to say.

"Kelly has agreed to join us for our small dinner party this evening. And of course, I will hold you to your commitment to attend, Theo," Madison looked pointedly at the handsome man astride beside her husband as she said it. Theo's face didn't betray anything.

"I will be there," Theodore said smoothly. "Until this evening, Miss Collins," he nodded to Kelly, Madison, and Henry, and then trotted off his horse down the path. Kelly looked after him musingly, uncomfortably aware of the butterflies that had taken flight inside her stomach.

"I don't see how you've managed to garner an invitation from the Marchioness of Clydon." Kelly's mother said doubtfully. She had followed Kelly down the stairs and stood with her hand on the banister as a maid handed her daughter a pelisse that matched her dress, to ward of the chill of the evening.

"I told you, Mama, it was all a chance encounter. We happened upon each other in the park and became acquainted." Kelly ignored her mother's arched eyebrows as she smoothed her dress. "I thought you would be thrilled when you heard that Lord Alston would be in attendance."

"I am…I'm just not entirely sure this is appropriate," She said slowly. "I really should be chaperoning you."

"The Marchioness of Clydon will act as my chaperone, Mama. She has graciously offered to take me under her wing for the season and ensure that I get all the right introductions at the right places. She is perfectly respectable." Kelly added the last part upon seeing her mother's still skeptical face.

"I suppose so…but she does not have the reputation for being the most conventional lady," Claire frowned.

"Her husband is close friends with Lord Alston," Kelly said simply as she pulled on her gloves. "That alone will ensure that I encounter Lord Alston as often as possible. And if our plan is to work, I will need ample opportunities to convince him that I am worth marrying." She reminded her mother.

Claire's frown deepened. She reached out and took her daughter's hands in hers, pulling her to sit on the small bench that was against the wall of the entry hall. Kelly frowned too, confused by her mother's demeanor. "You are worth marrying, my dear. Please don't think…" her mother paused, sighing sadly, "Please do not think that you are not worth marrying. Any gentleman would be lucky to have you. These circumstances…I don't know why Lord Alston is refusing to honor the betrothal…"

"Mama, don't think a thing of it." Kelly squeezed her mother's hand. "I am well, and all shall work out with Lord Alston, you shall see." She forced herself to smile at her mother as she said the words, and sent up a silent prayer that she would be brave enough to make good on them.

With a last squeeze to her mother, Kelly set off in the waiting carriage for the London home of the Marquess and Marchioness of Clydon. As she

smoothed her pale turquoise skirts for the tenth time,
she went over her strategy again in her mind. She
must be accommodating, agreeable, and show Theo
that she would make a model wife. She would show
him that she would be perfectly suited to his needs, no
matter what they were. She would make it clear that
there was absolutely nothing in her character which
could give him cause to break the betrothal.
Smoothing her dress again, she hoped she could
manage it.

Theodore arrived a bit early, as he always tended
to do. The Warsham's butler admitted him with a
smile and bid him wait in the salon for the lord and
lady of the house. Henry joined him a few moments
later.

"I'm quite surprised you didn't beg off," Henry said
forthrightly as he poured himself and Theo a drink
from the crystal decanter on the sideboard.

"Better to meet the challenge head-on, I suppose,"
Theo said wryly as he accepted the drink. "Madison
can't think I'm oblivious to her antics."

"Of course not, I just don't think she cares what
you think," Henry smiled, "She doesn't care what I
think either if it makes you feel any better."

"It doesn't," Theo answered. "But she won't
succeed."

"Well, she can't very well fix you up with a woman
you're already engaged to, now can she?" he said with
a chuckle.

Theodore was about to answer that quip, but the
door opened to admit another guest. In all, the dinner
party was small, consisting of Henry and Madison,
Madison's elder sister Leonora and her husband Lord

Avery, Lord Christopher Bowden, an old friend of Madison's, Theodore, and of course Kelly. Kelly was the last to arrive, and by the time she did, Theodore was starting on his second drink.

Madison got up instantly to greet her, but Theodore hung back watching. Though she looked nervous when she came in, her smiled greeting to Madison was genuine. Her eyes scanned the room, and he knew the instant they landed on him. At first, she glanced away quickly, seemingly embarrassed that she had caught him staring at her. She paused for a second, and then raised her eyes calmly to his and slowly smiled. And then she looked away, focusing on Leonora and her husband as they were introduced to her by Madison.

"Who the devil is that?" Christopher said, coming to stand beside Theo, drink in hand. "I certainly would have noticed her before." The appreciation in his voice was clear.

"She hasn't been up to town in years," Henry supplied helpfully from the other side of Theo. "Miss Kelly Collins, daughter of the Baron of Middleborough."

"She's not married then? Lovely," Christopher raised his glass to take a sip but nearly spilled it on himself as Theo pushed past him without warning, storming in the other direction. "What was that about?" Christopher turned to Henry, who raised his eyebrows and shrugged slightly.

Theo could not put a name to it, but he was put off the moment he heard the tone of Christopher's voice. Perhaps it was because he had known Kelly nearly all of his life and felt a certain responsibility towards her, given their situation. He certainly didn't feel anything as petty as jealousy; they had hardly spoken to each other in years. He had been protecting Kelly since they were children, that must be the emotion surfacing now.

He had moved instinctively towards her, but now that he was near her he didn't know how to act. He didn't want to give her any undue encouragement or make her think he was interested, but he couldn't help being drawn to her. He did have to convince her he wasn't a worthy husband so she would turn her sights elsewhere, a task he might as well start now.

"Miss Collins," He said smoothly, inserting himself into the conversation. "As always, it is a pleasure to see you."

"Thank you, Lord Alston." Kelly smiled. "I believe you already know Lady Warsham's relatives, Lord and Lady Avery?"

"Indeed, it is good to see you both again," Theodore kissed Leonora's hand and shook Lord Avery's.

"How nice of you to join us, Lord Alston. Now that you are back in town the ladies can begin swooning once again." Leonora said with a cheeky smile. "I would probably swoon for him too if I wasn't a married lady." She said with a wink to Kelly.

"Alas, Lady Avery, now you know why I eschew the thought of marriage, for you are already taken," Theodore answered, hand over his heart for effect. Kelly couldn't help but be charmed by Theo's humor and wit. It had been so long since she had seen this side of Theo, and she felt a pleasant warmth spreading through her body in response.

Leonora, easily fifteen years his senior, laughed heartily. "I shall have to whisk you away immediately, Leonora, so you don't fall under his spell!" Her husband said with mock haste, pulling her towards the other side of the room.

Kelly and Theo both smiled as the other couple departed, but when their eyes came back to each other the expressions faded into awkwardness. Before either could say anything, the butler announced dinner was served. Politely Theo offered his arm, and Kelly accepted it as he led her into the dining room. *Here we go*, they both thought to themselves.

Chapter 6

"Do you like to travel, Miss Collins?" Leonora asked.

"I suppose so," Kelly answered thoughtfully. "Honestly, I haven't had much occasion to travel. But I have enjoyed all the traveling I've done so far and am eager to do more."

Theodore sighed inwardly. He had just given a rambling explanation of how much he traveled as a peer of the realm, how his responsibilities to his multiple estates meant he made several long journeys each year. He had cataloged and exaggerated the hardships of this travel as much as he thought would still be believable. And calm little Kelly Collins had smiled serenely and said she would like to travel more.

"Do you have many siblings, Miss Collins?" said Leonora.

"I do not. I had neighbors and friends I was close with, of course," Kelly felt Theodore stiffen to her left but she didn't look at him. "But I always wanted brothers and sisters."

"You have to take the bad with the good. Look at those shoes my devil of a sister, Meera, sent me!" Madison interjected. "Though I suppose Leonora isn't so bad."

"Thank you, dear sister." Leonora rolled her eyes.

"I think because I was the only child, I've always wanted many children of my own. A little troupe to run around and keep each other company, and of course for me to spoil." Kelly said with a smile.

Theodore saw his opportunity. "Of course, until they are old enough to go away to boarding school." He said. "You can't keep your children under your thumb forever."

"I do agree, going away to Harrow was the best thing that ever happened to me, getting away from all of my sisters." Henry put in with a chuckle.

"I will tell your sisters you said that!" Madison said with a grin.

"It builds character! It makes you a man, learning to take care of yourself and have some sense of responsibility," Henry said in his own defense.

"I most certainly agree," Theodore nodded, noting the look of dismay on Kelly's face. Perfect, he thought. It was the first time all evening she hadn't jumped to agree with him. "I shall certainly send my sons off to Harrow as soon as they're old enough."

"I must disagree. I know of one young man in particular who went away and came back changed much for the worse." As soon as she said it, Kelly wished she had not. Although to all the others it was just another addition to the conversation, Theodore was looking directly at her with a distinct frown on his face.

"What do you mean?" Madison asked innocently.

Kelly swallowed and tried to keep her tone light, in keeping with the conversation. "You know how some of those schools are; they knock the spirit right out of the boys. Teaching them to be so straight-laced and proper, by the time they come home you hardly know who they are."

"But they must learn to behave properly at some point. They'll never learn everything at their mother's skirts." Theo said the comment to the table generally, but his gaze had not shifted from Kelly.

"Proper behavior can be taught at home." Kelly disagreed, trying hard to keep her voice from betraying her emotions and not entirely succeeding.

"They have to learn to be men," Theo said shortly.

Kelly opened her mouth to retort, and then closed it. Under the table, her hands were balled into fists. The pain in her chest was so real it felt as fresh as that moment on the steps almost ten years ago. The day that the Theo of her youth, friend and confidant, had been replaced by the stoic younger version of the man now sitting before her. "Of course, you are right, my lord." She said stiffly.

The conversation turned to other topics, and Kelly busied herself playing with the food on her plate. So much for being pliant and agreeable, she thought. But she couldn't help herself. The idea of her own sons being sent away, coming back as taciturn, emotionless young men made her go cold inside. The Theo she had adored had been taken from her in just that way.

Theo could see that she was almost in tears, but he couldn't understand why. He had seized upon the topic because he wanted to give an example of how they were not suited to one another. He had not expected the visceral emotional reaction from Kelly, which seemed to spring directly from him. Why did she seem so hurt? What had he ever done to hurt her? All he had ever done since they were small children was look out for her! Even now, as Christopher Bowden fawned over her and tried to make her laugh, all he wanted to do was rip the other man's head off.

"Miss Collins, there is a famous quartet putting on a public concert tomorrow afternoon. I would be honored if you would allow me to escort you." Christopher Bowden said with a charming smile. He had been showering her with attention all night, and while it was very flattering it made her objective of getting Theo to warm up to her all the more challenging. Though she had botched that well enough on her own.

The meal had finished and the small party had adjourned to the parlor for more drinks and conversation. Kelly had not gotten back up the nerve to pursue Theodore again after their heated exchange at the table. Chatting with Christopher Bowden had provided an enjoyable diversion, but Kelly knew that agreeing to go with him would be dangerously close to courting, and certainly wouldn't give Theo the right idea. "I'm sorry Lord Bowden, but my mother would never permit me such an outing without a chaperone." She said what she hoped was a kind but not encouraging smile.

"Then please bring one, by all means. Your mother is more than welcome to attend as your chaperone." He said accommodatingly. Lord Bowden was an exceptionally handsome man, with golden hair and seawater blue eyes. Kelly could see how a young woman would be easily charmed by him, and she sensed from his easy confidence that he was used to having his way with women. Despite this, she felt no real attraction to him. His persuasive blue eyes just made her think of Theo's brighter, more intense ones.

"I cannot," She said again, but she could feel herself starting to stumble over her words. In the eyes of propriety, there was no reason for her to refuse. But she could not accept or it would certainly give Theo the wrong idea. "I…please forgive me, I…my…"

"What Miss Collins means to say is that her fiancé would be most distressed if she were to accept your invitation," Theo said coolly. He had been watching Christopher's flattering attentions to Kelly all night and he had now had enough.

"Fiancé? Miss Collins, I had no idea you were betrothed." Christopher said with confusion.

"It is a long-standing family arrangement." Kelly managed to say.

"Forgive me, but perhaps you would still consider my offer? I should very much like to further our acquaintance if things are not entirely finalized with your betrothed." The young man pressed on, flashing his charming smile.

"My fiancée will not be going with you to the concert, Christopher," Theo said firmly. It took a moment for the words to set in before he realized what he had done. Inwardly he groaned, though he knew it was only a matter of time before all assembled would have learned the truth through other sources.

"Your fiancée? Hell, Theo, if she was your betrothed why didn't you just say so before?" Christopher said in astonishment. "Pardon my language, Miss Collins."

"Betrothed!?" Madison shrieked. Somehow, she had managed to lock in on that word even from across the room where she was supposedly engaged in another conversation. All of the eyes in the room were suddenly on Theo and Kelly. Madison's face was a mixture of shock and delight, while Henry chuckled to himself and took a swig of his brandy. "Theodore, did you say that you and Kelly are betrothed?" Madison managed to say, a disbelieving smile taking over her face.

"Miss Collins and I have been engaged since we were young children," Theodore said tightly. He could feel Kelly tensing next to him, and even as he instinctively moved closer to her he cursed himself for the impulse. It seemed like his legendary control had deserted him tonight.

"Why didn't you say anything earlier? This is marvelous!" Madison crossed the room and clasped Kelly's hands in excitement.

"We wanted to give Miss Collins some time to adjust back to the city before we made a more public announcement," Theo said, making up the excuse and hoping it sounded plausible. He took one of Kelly's hands out of Madison's and firmly drew her away. "If you'll excuse us for just a moment, Madison, I'd like a more private word with my fiancée?"

"Of course, of course!" Madison said, beaming. She ushered them into the adjoining room, amidst congratulations from the other attendees. She paused at the door in indecision and then winked at Theo. "I'll leave this door partially open, for the sake of propriety."

Kelly stared after her in stunned silence. Theo rolled his eyes, "It's not like I'm going to ravage you with a room of people ten feet away." He said under his breath. He let go of her hand and took a few steps back from her, crossing his arms. "I did not mean for our…relationship to become known like that."

Kelly took a deep breath. "Of course, my lord," she said. Y*ou didn't want it known at all*, she thought.

"I don't usually lose control of my temper like that." He said as he started pacing.

"I understand, my lord." She said calmly. *Usually, you are too calm and controlled.*

"I suppose I couldn't keep it quiet forever, now that you are in town."

"I suppose not." She nodded. *That was the whole point of my coming here.*

His face creased into a frown as he walked the perimeter of the room. "Madison will make sure everyone knows, she's happy as a cat that's found the cream."

"If you say so, my lord." Kelly agreed.

"Damn it, Kelly, don't you have anything more to say than that?" He snapped, turning quickly to face her.

"I thought you didn't lose your temper often?" She said with a smug smile.

Despite himself, Theo felt his frown melt and he chuckled. "You always were a mouthy little thing." He said.

"I think you'll find I'm quite agreeable," Kelly said sweetly.

"Too damned agreeable," He said, eyebrows raised. "What exactly are you playing at, Miss Collins?"

"Nothing at all," Kelly said innocently, but she felt the melting pressure of his eyes on her. When had he become so handsome? She thought to herself. Suddenly she was very aware of how alone they were, even with the door to the next room just a few feet away.

He had always been attractive, but as a man, those brilliant blue eyes paired with his thick dark hair had become a lethal combination. No wonder everyone is so surprised he is engaged to me, she thought; I must look like a country mouse in comparison.

"I am trying to be a perfectly accommodating fiancée." She said, taking a step back from him this time, away from his overwhelming masculinity.

"You were never a particularly accommodating child," Theo said, stepping closer to her.

"I have changed." She said truthfully. She wasn't the same carefree child she had been. The stakes were much higher now, and she had to grow up and act accordingly.

"Perhaps," Theo said slowly, his next step bringing them close enough to touch. "But perhaps not too much," he said quietly, brushing away a tendril of hair that had fallen across her cheek. Kelly saw the emotion on his face, though she couldn't identify it. It seemed almost like yearning, but for what? Any such display of emotion was unusual from Theo, let alone anything that made him seem vulnerable. "You can still see your freckles if you look closely." He said softly.

It was as if all the air had rushed out of her body and she had neither strength nor will to draw another breath. Kelly was frozen to the spot, her skin tingling where he had touched it. His face was close to hers, only a few inches separating them. And then he took a sudden and distinct step back. Kelly felt the air rush back to her lungs, and she turned away from him so he wouldn't see the emotions rushing across her face. "What do we do now?" She said, more to herself than to him.

"Between Countess Crawford and our friend Madison, the whole *ton* will know of our association very shortly." The mask of calm composure had dropped back over Theo.

"Yes, I can see that." Kelly agreed. "We are betrothed."

"Kelly, I…." Theo started and then stopped, trying out the words in his mind. "I'm not a suitable husband. I will not make a good husband for you."

Kelly frowned. "Whatever do you mean? I shall be amenable to your needs, whatever they may be."

"I'm sure you would, Kelly, but I would not make a good husband to anyone. Marriage is not for me." He said. Kelly was perplexed. What a strange statement, from a peer of the realm.

"But you must marry eventually. I assure you, I will be a thoughtful and accommodating wife. I am ready." She said, hoping her desperation wasn't as evident as it felt.

"Kelly, I'm not going to change my mind about this."

"Then I suppose we are at an impasse, for neither am I. You must marry eventually, and I am your betrothed." Kelly said firmly. Riding the wave of confidence flowing through her, she took a step towards him, forgetting the space she had purposefully placed between them just moments earlier. "Please, Theodore, let me show you. I will be no burden to you, no trouble at all, truly,"

She was cut off abruptly as she felt Theo reach out and drag her to him. Before she was aware of what was happening, his lips were on hers in a crushing kiss. Crushing was the word she thought of to describe it later; as he kissed her, all thoughts tumbled from her head.

Kelly had never been kissed by anyone before. His mouth was somehow hard and yet velvety soft at the same time. Her lips tingled at the sensation of his rubbing against hers, and the tingling seemed to spread through her chest, where her heart had started pounding wildly. The feelings were intensely pleasurable, so much more so than Kelly had ever imagined a kiss could be.

The gentle pressure of his tongue urged her lips apart, and she was startled when she felt his tongue enter her mouth. Her abrupt response seemed to startle Theo back to reality. He pulled away from her slightly but didn't release her arms. He dragged in a ragged breath before saying softly: "You are more trouble than you know."

Before she could ask him what he meant, he released her arms and returned to the adjoining room.

Chapter 7

Wenn Theo rejoined the group, he noted the other guests' careful determination not to look at him but he ignored it. He made a quick excuse to Madison and then he departed without further delay before Kelly could even reenter the room. He knew his return to the room without her, followed by his immediate departure, did not cast their relationship in the best light. Blast it, he thought to himself. It was probably for the better that it looked like they were at odds. It would make it all the more believable when they publicly ended their betrothal.

Stepping into his carriage, he cursed his impulsiveness. Publicly claiming Kelly Collins as his fiancée and then kissing her soundly was exactly the opposite of what he had intended. But when she stood there, practically begging him to be her husband, he couldn't help himself. He couldn't recall the last time he had lost control like that. He prided himself on keeping a tight leash on his emotions. In his home, his father had made it a prerequisite for survival. After a certain amount of time, keeping himself under tight control had become completely second nature.

But she was so damn irresistible. It would be so much easier to shrug her off if she had been another one of those empty-headed women that Madison was continually trying to foist upon him. But this was Kelly. She possessed keen intelligence, deeply rooted stubbornness and determination, and the most enticing brown eyes that one easily became lost in. He groaned and raked his hand through his hair.

He would have to appeal to her rational side, he told himself. He would have to logically lay out the reasons they could not be wed and convince her of the fact. There could be no more dancing around it, and he should have known better from the beginning. The best way to deal with Kelly would be to tell her straight out what a horrible husband he would be.

The next morning was bright and sunny. It was the perfect day for a drive in the park, which was exactly the sort of opportunity that Theodore had hoped for to enact his newest plan of action. He knocked firmly on the door of the townhouse and was admitted quickly to the parlor. "Lady Collins will be with you very shortly." The butler said with a short bow.

"Lord Alston is here?" Kelly repeated in disbelief. She was frozen with her fork halfway to her mouth, a bit of egg threatening comically to fall back to her plate. "You're sure?"

"Quite sure, my lady. He asked to speak with you, Lady Collins," the butler said, addressing Kelly's mother. Claire's lips were pursed and her brows furrowed. She was just as baffled as Kelly at the sudden development. But then she awakened to action.

"Well, we certainly shouldn't keep him waiting." She bustled to her feet, patting her hair and straightening her bodice as she stood. "Kelly, do straighten yourself up and then come along, we must not waste this opportunity." She said, following the butler from the dining room.

Kelly sat in stunned silence. After the events of the previous evening, Kelly had no idea what to make of Theodore's sudden appearance. Just the thought of last night made her cheeks hot and her lips tingle. No one had ever treated her the way that Theo had. One minute he was kissing her, which was surely a positive sign, and the next he had disappeared altogether, which was decidedly negative. Perhaps he had not enjoyed kissing her. The thought saddened her unexplainably.

Had he come to apologize? It didn't seem likely. Theo had never been the type to apologize easily. He was much too arrogant for that. Cautiously, she walked towards the parlor, straining to hear what her mother and Theo were saying. Her mother sounded quite excited. Slowly she pushed open the door.

"Kelly! There you are!" Her mother almost squealed. She reached for Kelly's hand and drew her into the room. "Lord Alston has come to ask you to go for a drive in the park with him. Doesn't that sound lovely?" She said, beaming.

Theodore smiled charmingly, but Kelly hesitated. She tried to discern what his intention might be but his guarded smile betrayed nothing. She nodded slowly, answering politely "Of course, Mama. But don't you think you ought to accompany us, as a chaperone?"

"Oh, my dear, a drive through the busy park in an open carriage can hardly do any harm. I think it would be a nice time for you two to further renew your acquaintance." Claire smiled meaningfully at her daughter. "Now run along and fetch your bonnet so you do not keep Lord Alston waiting."

Although suspicious of Theodore's intentions, Kelly could hardly refuse. She did as her mother asked and ten minutes later, Theodore had handed Kelly up into the seat of his coach, taken the reigns, and they had departed from the townhouse amid Claire Collins' enthusiastic waves. Theodore was startlingly aware of Kelly's body on the seat only mere inches away from him. He drove the carriage carefully so that no jar or sudden bump would cause his body to touch hers accidentally. The consequences of that, he feared, would not be good for either of their reputations. After last night, he knew his body could not be trusted when it came to Kelly.

Kelly could feel the heat of Theo's body pulling her like a magnet. She carefully folded her hands in her lap and looked ahead, completely unsure of how to begin a conversation with him when her every thought made her recall their last encounter. Fortunately, Theo spared her the awkwardness of having to break the silence.

"Miss Collins, I would like to discuss matters with you frankly." He said as he steered the carriage onto the main path. "I see no reason for us to be at odds; we have known one another for the greater part of our lives, and we should be able to converse now as adults."

"I suppose that is true," Kelly said, bemused by Theo's manner. She turned to look at him, but his gaze was focused determinedly ahead, unwilling to spare her even a glance.

"Excellent. I have considered our current arrangement, and concluded that the best course of action is to break off our engagement immediately." He said succinctly, without emotion.

Kelly felt her mouth fall open in a most undignified manner. "I…I…" She bit her lip in frustration at her damnable stuttering. "I…I fail to see how that could possibly be the best course of action." She managed to get out.

"I can see why you might be confused, given your current understanding of the situation. But I assure you, what once seemed a very suitable match is no longer beneficial to either side." He said patronizingly.

"Please, apprise me of the situation." She said sarcastically, though her intonation was lost on Theodore. He kept talking without hesitation.

"The reason for our union was to end once and for all the squabbles about the demarcation between our two estates. However, I firmly believe this is the squabble of unreasonable old men, not rational people like us. I will gladly redraw the line between our estates in a way that is to your complete satisfaction and allows us each to go our own way in our endeavors." He plowed on, trying to remain completely emotionless.

Kelly, on the other hand, was seething with emotion. Perhaps she should be devastated, but the only emotion coursing through her at the moment was disdain. A mere twelve hours ago he was kissing her in Madison's parlor, and now he was attempting to cast her off. However, before she could gather herself enough to respond, Theodore continued his onslaught.

"Furthermore, I am in no way an ideal husband. I am extremely independent and will not submit myself to being pestered about when I shall be home, or what functions I shall attend, or the like. I have an able-bodied housekeeper, butler, and valet and have no need of a wife to meddle in my affairs. Marriage is a ghastly arrangement and I will avoid it for as long as possible."

"Wh…What about heirs? Do you think you can beget those independently as well?" She managed to interject.

"That is a matter to be dealt with far down the road." He responded dismissively.

"May I speak now, my lord?" She said softly.

"Of course, Miss Collins," He smiled, pleased at her calm and, as he interpreted it, resigned manner.

Kelly took a determined breath. "First of all, Lord Alston, let me inform you that there is no way in which you could redraw the boundary lines between our estates which would satisfy me short of erasing the line altogether and surrendering your lands to me completely. I can also assure you that I have much less frivolous things to worry about than what time you return home or which party you attend. I would like nothing more than to return to my home and allow your housekeeper, butler, and valet to continue to manage your affairs. And lastly, no matter how loudly you protest it you will need to marry eventually to ensure you have someone to pass that lofty title on to in the future. Since you are so supremely rational, I will leave you now to consider the situation, as you so delicately call it." Reaching for the reigns, Kelly gave a sharp yank that pulled the horses to a halt. Without assistance, she stepped down from the carriage and walked away.

Chapter 8

*K*elly did not look back over her shoulder, but she knew the instant that Theodore came to his senses or some semblance of them, because she heard him jump down from the carriage and start after her. She was seething with fury. How dare he speak to her in such a way? How dare he be so dismissive of his responsibility to her? How dare he treat her beloved home as if it was something to be bargained over? He was the same cold, taciturn young man he had been for so many years. She had been foolish to be deceived into thinking otherwise by his accidental displays of feeling.

"Miss Collins, you cannot walk alone through the park like this. It isn't proper. Please allow me to escort you home." Theodore called to her as he closed the steps between them.

"Do you think our yelling at one another as we ride through the park is preferable?" She said without sparing him a glance or slowing her pace.

"Damn it, Kelly, you are being ridiculous. Get back in the carriage." He had caught up with her now and was matching her brisk pace.

"I will not. I have been embarrassed enough for one morning." She said stubbornly.

"And you think that storming through the park while I trail behind you shouting won't embarrass you or harm your reputation further?"

"Not nearly as much harm as will be done to my reputation when you throw me over publicly," She snapped. She felt the tears threatening, but she bit them back determinedly.

"You can be the one to call of the engagement. You can blame it entirely on me; make up whatever defect you desire as your excuse. I can withstand whatever the *ton* wants to think or say about me." Theo answered.

She stopped abruptly and threw her hands up in the air. "I can't call off the engagement!" Kelly forced herself to take a couple of deep breaths before she continued. There didn't seem to be any use in trying to keep her motivations secret any longer. She sighed in defeat. "Theodore, you want us to be honest and rational with one another, and so I shall be. The situation is as follows: my family needs this marriage to happen or we will lose the estate completely. There is no money left. I do not know all the details of how the financial situation became so dire, but it doesn't really matter. The stipulations of the marriage contract agreed to by our fathers would ensure that the estate is preserved. I have no dowry to entice another suitor; this is my only option. *You* are my only option."

Theodore stared at her. He had no idea what to say; of all the possible reactions, the chain of events which had left him standing in the park, yards away from his carriage and face to face with Kelly, hands on her hips and heart in her eyes, was not what he had expected. After a few moments, Kelly turned away and put one hand to her mouth, clearly trying to regain her composure.

Taking stock of the odd looks they were getting from passersby, Theo kept his face and voice calm and neutral. "Thank you for your honesty, Miss Collins. Now please, allow me to escort you back to the carriage." He held out his hand. The despair in Kelly's eyes as she turned back to him almost broke his resolve. She seemed to consider for a moment whether she should accept his offer, but after a moment she nodded silently and took his hand.

"I apologize for making a scene," Kelly said hollowly once she was seated again in the carriage. "I just don't know what I'm going to do." She whispered, more to herself than to him. Theo almost groaned out loud. Lord, it was like she was cutting him into tiny little pieces. How was it possible that he felt the villain in this story? How was any of this his fault?

They sat in silence as Theo drove the carriage back towards the Collins' residence. Kelly was angry with herself for showing her hand, as it was, so quickly. However, she was also relieved that all of the cards were on the table. She couldn't put on a false façade around people, and especially not around Theo himself. She certainly hadn't succeeded at it over the past few days. At least this way, Theo did not doubt her intentions and whatever was going to happen could be decided with clear consciences on both sides. The jolt of the carriage as it came to a stop broke her train of thought.

Theodore hopped down and came around to her side of the carriage to help her down. "Thank you for the excursion," Kelly said politely as she climbed down. She turned to walk inside.

"Kelly…" Theodore did not release her hand, preventing her from leaving. Her hand seemed so small in comparison to his, almost childlike. But there was also an underlying strength: in the set of her eyes, the posture of her body, the way she held his hand firmly even now. He was overwhelmed by a desire to take care of her, to take away that burden which she carried. "There is a solution to this that will satisfy both of our needs and desires, I am certain of it. I need some time to think on it, but I promise, you do not have to solve this on your own." On a sudden and uncharacteristic impulse, he brought her hand to his lips and kissed it softly.

Kelly felt herself begin to melt in response, but before she could say a word Theo released her and climbed back aboard his carriage. "I will see you again soon," He said, tipping his hat and snapping the reigns smartly to start down the street. Kelly watched the carriage move away and disappear down the corner.

"You're back!" Kelly's mother cried from the doorway. Kelly wondered how long she had been watching. "How did it go, darling? Lord Alston seemed quite affectionate with you!" She said excitedly, and then seemed to reflect on that. "Not too affectionate, I hope."

Kelly sighed at her mother's concern. "It was all quite proper, Mama, I assure you."

"He will call again! That certainly means things are moving in the right direction!" Claire continued, confirming that she had indeed been eavesdropping, but had not heard the entire conversation.

"I'm not certain what it means," Kelly said, taking one last look down the street where the carriage had disappeared.

Chapter 9

*T*wo full days passed and Kelly did not see nor hear from Theodore. In that space of time, she attended an afternoon tea, an evening soiree, and another ball. While she had encountered her new friend Madison at two of these events, and her husband Lord Warsham at one, Theodore was absent. However, as absent as he was from her life physically, he made constant appearances in her conversations. The word of their betrothal was out, and it was always the first thing someone remarked about upon making her acquaintance.

"I never thought that boy would settle down! Smart of his father to arrange it all ahead of time so it was taken care of," the old Lady Dewsbury commented to her elderly friend, Lady Sharpton. Kelly was uncertain whether this comment was meant to be heard by her or not, so she decided to ignore it. She wasn't offended; she had heard everything from complete surprise to thinly veiled disdain that such an *unknown* had been able to take one of the *ton's* most eligible bachelors off the market. Silly old ladies did not worry her; what did was that she hadn't heard a peep from Theodore. Was he reconsidering his promise to aid her? Was he planning on throwing her over and just trying to get up the courage to do it?

Kelly stifled a yawn as piano music began to fill the room. She was attending a concert being given by the daughters of Lord and Lady Atwell. Tomorrow, she promised herself, she would sleep in late and beg off any afternoon entertainments her mother tried to foist upon her. The late hours of city life, such a departure from the quiet tempo of days in the country, were beginning to catch up with her. Letting the music flow over her, she felt her eyes start to drift shut just as someone took the seat next to her.

"We need to talk," Theodore whispered into her ear, jolting her awake. As she tried to clear her mind, she realized she had grabbed his hand in her surprise. The current between them was electric. Her whole body started to heat. Unsure of herself and these strange feelings, she began to let go, but Theodore's grip tightened. "Come with me." He whispered. Silently, he drew her to her feet. They were seated near the back of the room, and as they stood the Atwell daughters began a jaunty piano piece that held everyone's attention. No one seemed to notice as Theo led Kelly quietly into the hallway.

"Lord Alston, I'm sure this is not appropriate. My mother will notice I am gone at any moment." Kelly admonished immediately.

"We'll only be gone a few minutes. Besides, as an engaged couple, we're allowed a bit more lenience." Theodore whispered. Kelly wasn't sure if she believed that, but she remained with him in the hall. "I've been thinking about our predicament."

"And have you arrived at some grand solution?" Kelly arched her delicate eyebrows doubtfully.

"Not yet," Theodore frowned, annoyed at his awareness of her and of his body's physical response. They were outside of the music room in the wide hallway, but their bodies were close together so they could hear each other's whispers. Only inches separated them, and Theo had to do everything in his power to keep himself from closing that distance. Kelly, however, seemed unaffected. She crossed her arms and looked at him expectantly. "I will come up with something. In the meantime, we will continue the charade of being engaged…"

"It's not a charade," Kelly protested. "We are engaged! Or have you forgotten?"

"You know what I mean. We will see each other socially, polite exchanges, and so on. But not too much; we don't want to appear so smitten that when we call things off, people are shocked."

"When we call things off? Theo, I don't think that's being realistic…" Theo cut off her worried response.

"Look, I need more time to figure this out." He took her hand and squeezed it. "I promise I will fix this, Kelly. Haven't I always protected you?" Kelly held her breath. She nodded silently.

"We should return now. I will go in first, you follow me in a few moments." He released her hand and stepped back towards the concert. "I will find a way to make both of us happy." He said.

As he left her standing there, Kelly had the feeling that the answer to what would make her happy was getting more complicated by the moment. Once she had been honest with him about her plight, his aloofness had seemed to fade and this other side of him had emerged. This Theo, reassuring, smiling, was completely disarming. So close to the Theo she had known, yet she was afraid to trust his warm demeanor.

When she reentered the room and took her seat, she did not see Theodore. She tried to quell the little trill of disappointment that popped up and focus on the music. Of course, she was so wrapped up in her own musings that she barely noticed what was happening around her, and before she realized it the guests around her were applauding and beginning to converse. The performance had ended.

"Well, Miss Hailey Atwell is most talented on the piano, but Miss Isabella Atwell certainly leaves much to be desired." Lady Dewsbury turned and said to Lady Sharpton. Rolling her eyes, Kelly excused herself from the gossipy old ladies. Her mother was not far away, chatting amiably with the Earl of Kerrick. She didn't think Madison was present, and Theodore seemed to have disappeared.

"Miss Collins, it is a pleasure to see you again!" Christopher, Lord Bowden emerged from the gathered crowd, took her hand, and smiled widely.

"And you, my lord." Kelly returned his smile, grateful to have someone to talk to other than her mother or the old ladies.

"Is your fiancé accompanying you this evening?" Lord Bowden asked, glancing around warily.

"I am here with my mother, Lady Collins," Kelly answered, since Theodore seemed to have disappeared.

"I'm glad to hear it," Lord Bowden said with an impish grin. "He was making it very difficult to have even the briefest of conversations with you."

"Lord Bowden," Kelly scoffed, "you shouldn't tease."

"Please, call me Christopher." He returned, his smile deepening.

"Now that would be entirely improper." But Kelly couldn't help but chuckle and return his smile. She did enjoy Christopher, who was quick to make a joke and quick to smile. He was much more straightforward than Theo. And although she knew it could go nowhere, and she didn't want it to go anywhere, she was enjoying his attention. She noted that other guests were observing them, perhaps a little questioningly. It seemed without even actively trying, she was perpetuating Theodore's desired impression that their attachment was not set in stone.

From across the room, Theodore watched Kelly and Christopher closely. He heard Kelly's tinkling laugh across the large, crowded room as if it were the only sound. Damn, this should not bother him. This was exactly what he wanted – for people to think that his and Kelly's engagement was a sham cooked up by their parents, which would understandably be undone now that they were both adults. Did she have to make it look so convincing? Her mouth partially open, like she was waiting on bated breath for Christopher's next statement. It did not matter, he told himself. She was not his to worry about. And even so, Christopher could be a suitable match for her. He was not exceptionally wealthy, but his family was comfortable. She wouldn't want for anything as his wife. *Christopher's wife?* Theo had an almost physical reaction to the thought.

She laughed again, putting her hand prettily to her chest. Christopher leaned over and put his hand familiarly on her arm while he whispered something close to her ear. Theo felt an intense burning spark to life in his gut. *Enough.*

Chapter 10

Kelly was taking a steadying sip of her punch, laughter still in her eyes, when she noticed that Christopher's smile had faded and he had stiffened.

"Lord Alston, good evening." She heard him say formally. And then she was aware of the presence behind her. She felt a possessive hand at the small of her back, and the emanating heat of his body close to hers.

"Good evening to you, Lord Bowden." Theodore said coolly, "I see you have been keeping my fiancée entertained while I was delayed. Thank you for that." His hand was like a brand where it rested on her back. Kelly felt like the heat was taking over her body. "May I be let in on the joke, my love?" He said casually.

Kelly stared at him dumbly. *My love?* Had he taken leave of his senses?

Christopher came to her rescue. "I was relating a rather embarrassing story of a childhood prank gone awry, my lord."

"How charming. Did you know that Miss Collins and I grew up together? We have so many fondly shared memories from our childhood. Do you remember the time, Kelly, when that fish got ahold of your pole and dragged you into the pond?" The use of her given name was not lost on Kelly, nor the familiarity that it implied.

Kelly's eyes narrowed. "As I recall, Lord Alston, it was your fishing pole. And you asked me to stand watch on it while you tried your hand at catching a fish with your bare hands; an endeavor which landed you in the pond as well, if I remember correctly."

"Ah, so it was," Theo admitted, flashing a charming smile meant for Kelly alone and looking rather intently into her eyes.

"Please excuse me, I don't wish to intrude." Christopher Bowden gave a small bow and quickly departed. Theo continued to smile adoringly until he was well away.

"You, well...you..." Kelly began, only to be interrupted.

"Thank goodness he finally took his leave," Theo said in a clipped tone.

"Only because you made him feel so awkward, standing here staring at me like a lovesick fool!" Kelly bit out.

"Isn't that what fiancés are supposed to do?" He asked mockingly.

"One minute you say we should act detached, only polite with one another. Then the next you are here carrying on. What is the matter with you?" She asked, stepping away from him and crossing her arms.

"I did not say anything that was not true." Theodore defended.

"But you could have talked about anything! Instead, you tell a story clearly meant to make Lord Bowden feel excluded and go away."

"That is because I wanted him to go away!" His tone started to elevate.

"Why? We were having a perfectly amicable conversation." Kelly raised her eyebrows expectantly.

"He was far too interested in you, an already betrothed woman."

"A farce of a betrothal, as you are fond of reminding me. Perhaps he has caught on to that, which is exactly what you wanted, isn't it?"

"Stay away from him, Kelly." His dark tone took Kelly aback. She paused for a second. Why did this matter to him so much?

"I…you aren't being fair, Theodore, I…well…" She stammered.

"It is time you were returned to your mother." And just like that, the calm, cool veneer was back in place. Theodore took her arm and led her back to Claire Collins. He gave a short bow to her mother and placed a polite kiss on the top of her hand. "Good evening, Miss Collins." And then he left, leaving Kelly feeling even more perplexed than she had at the start of the evening.

Chapter 11

*T*heodore was overwhelmed at his idiocy. He should have left that damnable party directly after his first conversation with Kelly. That had been his only reason for attending. He should not have allowed himself to watch her or to jealously intervene in her conversation with Christopher Bowden. His father would have mocked him mercilessly for his lack of self-control. He would have scolded him; lectured him about the impropriety and indignity of not having complete control of one's actions.

He could feel a headache forming as he mounted the stairs to his townhouse. Rubbing absently at his temples, he missed noticing the other carriage pulled up in front as he entered.

"My lord," His butler opened the door, taking his coat from him. "My lord, her ladyship…" The older man tried to get the warning out, but he was too late.

"Theodore!"

Theo winced as he turned to the stately figure seated regally on his parlor sofa. "Mother," he managed by way of a greeting.

"You are home earlier than I expected! Your butler told me that you were attending a music concert at the home of the Lord and Lady Atwell. After that treat, I expected you would retire to your gentleman's club to help your ears recover." She said with a shrewd smile. She stood and embraced him, a show of affection that Theodore accepted readily. There were few people he was close to in his life: his friend, Henry Warsham, whom he had known since his school days at Harrow and who had helped divert his attention from his unhappy home; his mother, who had endured his father's cold demeanor stoically alongside him; and once upon a time, the shining, young, Kelly Collins.

"It is a pleasure to see you Mother, though a bit of a surprise." He pulled back and looked her over with a critical gaze. Like her son, she was tall. Age had stooped her height only slightly, and she still had a bearing that garnered attention in any room. Her gray hair was coiffed fashionably, and though she was not young she also wouldn't have been described by anyone as feeble or elderly. But Theo thought he detected strain around her eyes, an air of worry, something he had not seen since his father had passed away. "Are you alright?" He asked.

Lady Eleanor Alston waved her hand dismissively. "Of course, of course. I was just starting to feel a bit bored by myself out in the country. It does get a bit tedious without you around." Theo felt a twinge of guilt; he should have made more of a point to visit her during his extended sojourn in London. Though her stature was still tall and erect and her demeanor regal as a queen's, he knew she was not entirely honest with him about the state of her health. He paid all of her bills, and the doctor had visited more times than could be easily explained away.

"So, do tell me, Theo," She said, seating herself on the sofa and motioning for him to join her "Whatever enticed you to attend a musical concert given by two debutantes? It does not seem like your usual entertainment." She eyed him knowingly.

"I assure you it was not for the dazzling musical performance." He answered evasively.

"It wouldn't be because a certain Miss Collins was in attendance, would it?" She said, a devious glint in her eye. Theo sighed and leaned back on the sofa, crossing his arms. It seemed his mother had an altogether different reason for coming to town.

"It seems you are not so bored out there in the country as you would let on." He said dryly.

"Just because one is out of town does not mean one needs to be out of touch. I enjoy a healthy correspondence with several friends who keep me apprised of the goings-on here in London. In any case, you are changing the subject."

Theo rolled his eyes. "Mother, I can assure you nothing is going on here that necessitated your sudden journey."

"I disagree." She said firmly. "I have it on good authority that Miss Collins is here in London making the societal rounds, and that your betrothal is public knowledge. So really, my purpose in being here is to help you set the date and plan the nuptials."

Theo actually laughed out loud. "There will be no nuptials, Mother."

"Oh Theodore, of course there will be. You have shied away from this long enough. The poor girl has been of age for three years now. It's time to have this whole thing settled so that you can work on giving me some grandchildren." Her eyes twinkled at the thought.

"You are going to have to wait for that, mother. I assure you, I have no intention of wedding Miss Collins."

She frowned. "And why not? You have known one another since you were children."

"Exactly. And just because our fathers made a silly arrangement when we were children does not bind us inextricably as adults." His face was set in a firm line. Eleanor's frown deepened.

"Well you certainly haven't expressed interest in any other young ladies, so what is the problem with Miss Collins? You both always seemed to get on so well."

"There is nothing wrong with Miss Collins," Even as he said it, the vision of Kelly's pretty face popped into his mind; her intelligent brown eyes, her enticing pink lips. Forcing the image from his head, he continued. "I do not wish to be married at all."

"You don't wish to be married." His mother repeated. "That is utterly ridiculous, Theodore. You have a duty to marry and produce an heir to continue our family line. And secondly, you will find happiness in marriage…"

"No," he cut her off and stood abruptly. Eleanor sat on the sofa, staring after him as he crossed to the window and stared out. She could read the stiff lines of his body; she knew her son well enough to sense his resoluteness. "I am perfectly happy as I am.

Eventually, an heir will be needed, that is not in dispute. But not now; I am not ready for marriage and the trials it will entail."

Then Eleanor understood. She stood, and placed a gentle hand upon her son's shoulder. "Your marriage to Miss Collins will not be like your father and I's." She said quietly.

Theodore stiffened. He stood there for several moments, staring out the window. "I have made up my mind on this, Mother." He said with finality. He gave her hand a quick squeeze, and then he left.

Staring after him, Eleanor shook her head sadly. "Oh Theodore, you're going to need all the help you can get."

Chapter 12

*I*t was already mid-morning when Theodore descended the stairs of his townhouse the next day. As he sought out something to eat, he heard the clinking of teacups and the sound of women's laughter from the parlor. His mother was wasting no time renewing acquaintances, it would appear. Hoping to escape their notice, he moved quietly towards the front door.

"Theodore, do come in and say good morning." His mother called. He gritted his teeth. How were mothers always so keenly aware? Forcing a polite smile on his face, he prepared to meet one of his mother's batty old friends. Pushing open the parlor door, he did a quick double-take.

"Good morning, Theodore!" Madison said with a wide smile. She was seated on the sofa, a teacup in her hand, appearing to get on famously with his mother.

"Good morning to you, Madison. Mother," he nodded his greetings. "I did not know the two of you were acquainted."

"Well, we weren't, until today," Madison answered, her smile getting even broader if that was possible.

"You have always been such good friends with Lady Warsham's husband, it seemed remiss that I had not met his lovely wife. I sent around a note last night inviting her for tea this morning and she graciously agreed." His mother explained. It was perfectly reasonable, but Theo was not fully convinced.

"I was just telling your mother how much I've come to enjoy your Kelly's company. That is, Miss Collins," Madison corrected with a small laugh. "I beg your pardon, with our friendship I already think of her as Kelly. I'm sure you've all known each other for so long that you are on familiar terms as well."

Theodore did not like this one bit. He had known what Madison had on her mind from the first moment she clapped eyes on Kelly. He most definitely did not need her scheming with his mother. When Theodore did not respond to Madison, his mother jumped in.

"It has been several years since I have seen Miss Collins. Not since Theodore's father passed on. I am looking forward to getting to know the young woman she has become."

"You will not be disappointed," Madison said loyally.

Oh Lord, Theodore groaned inwardly. This was a disaster. Madison and his mother would have him wedded and bedded before the month was out. Again, the image of Kelly Collins came unbidden, this time of her lying on a bed, that charming little smile on her lips in invitation... He cleared his head and schooled his features to match. *Enough of this*, he told himself again. He needed to get control of himself, and this situation, before both spiraled out of control.

Meanwhile, Kelly was enjoying a blissfully solitary morning in her parlor. Her mother was suffering a headache and remained abed. Kelly felt the slightest twinge of guilt at her enjoyment of her mother's indisposition, but it was quickly put aside as she reflected on the fact that for one peaceful day, she was free of the *ton*'s social engagements.

"Miss Collins, Lord Bowden to see you." Kelly nearly dropped the periodical she had been reading as the butler made his announcement. She sprang to her feet as the handsome Christopher Bowden entered the room, dropping into a deep if somewhat exaggerated bow.

"Lord Bowden, this is certainly a surprise." She managed to say.

"Miss Collins," he took her hand and planted a little kiss on it, then smiled at her. "I hope it is a pleasant surprise, at the very least?" He teased.

Kelly couldn't help her smile in return. "Indeed, it is not altogether displeasing." She matched his teasing grin.

"Your reluctance wounds me," He said, placing a hand to his heart and feigning a look of hurt. Kelly's laughter bubbled over again. "I certainly doubt that." She smiled and motioned for him to

sit in the chair opposite her. Resuming her seat, she asked, "Would you care for some tea, my lord?"

"Tea would be lovely." He answered with a charming smile. By the time Kelly rang for tea, her maid, clearly alerted by the butler, had entered the room to chaperone the social visit from an interested young man. Kelly wondered if someone had alerted her mother as well. She certainly would not approve of this caller, given that he was not Lord Alston.

"I apologize that our discussion was cut short last evening, Miss Collins. I wanted to let you know that I was certainly enjoying myself." He said, rather boldly in Kelly's opinion.

"Really, it is I who should apologize on behalf of Lord Alston. I'm sorry he was unkind to you." She said genuinely.

"Think nothing of it, he has always been rather unpleasant," Christopher said with a wink.

Kelly frowned. "He is not unpleasant." She said defensively. "I...he...there is nothing wrong with being well-composed." She heard herself say, disbelieving that the words had just come out of her own mouth. Was she really defending Theodore's controlled, contrived demeanor, the very thing that had frustrated her for so many years? But she was unexplainably put off to hear anyone criticizing him.

"I suppose not," Christopher said slowly, aware of the change in her tone. "I was merely commenting on..."

"Miss Collins, Lord Alston to see you." The butler announced at the door. This time, it was Christopher who shot to his feet. Theodore cut an impressive figure in the doorway, his dark hair complemented by his dark coat. Kelly had noticed over the past few meetings that he tended to favor dark colors. It made him look more severe and imposing, which she guessed was his reasoning. It didn't exactly make him an inviting figure. But it also had the unintended effect of making his dark brown hair look richer, and his startling blue eyes stand out even more noticeably.

He fixed those piercing blue eyes on Christopher Bowden. For a moment, Kelly thought she read anger in his eyes, but then it was gone and she wasn't sure it had ever been there. Really, what reason did he have to be angry anyway?

"Miss Collins, Lord Bowden," Theodore said formally. He bowed slightly to Christopher, before crossing to Kelly and claiming her hand. He placed a slow, deliberate kiss on her sensitive skin, and Kelly felt that same strange warmth spread through her body from the place where his lips touched her.

When he turned back to Christopher, his gaze and tone were cool and controlled. "Lord Bowden, if you would excuse us, I need to speak to my fiancée on a pressing personal matter."

Christopher looked from Theo to Kelly and back again. When Kelly did not object, he nodded hesitantly. "I hope to see you again soon, Miss Collins." He said forwardly, placing a kiss on her hand in much the same way Theodore had. Kelly waited for her body to tingle in response, but it did not. She gave him a small smile as she bid him goodbye.

"You have certainly had a busy morning," Theodore said when the other man had left. He turned to the maid, hovering protectively on the outskirts of the room. "As I said, I require a personal word with my fiancée." When the maid did not move, he continued more pointedly. "You may keep the door open and return to check on us as often as you'd like, but I do require private words with Miss Collins." The maid struggled with indecision, but in the end, she did as Theo bid her. Though he doubted that she had retreated any farther than a few feet outside the parlor door into the entrance hall.

"What is this about?" Kelly asked suspiciously.

"I have a plan," Theo said. Kelly's eyebrows shot up.

"I…what? Already? What could…could, you…" Theo held up his hand to cut her off.

"Hear me out, Miss Collins. We have known each other for many years. Indeed, we could call ourselves friends. Although we are friends, we have decided that we would not suit one another in marriage." Kelly wondered where this was going, but she didn't interrupt him. "As such, we have decided to call off our engagement, so that you might be able to find someone better suited."

"You are forgetting that I do not have a dowry." She managed to say.

"Yes, I have considered this. Given the duration of our friendship and our close familial ties, I will be happy to provide a dowry on your behalf."

Kelly's heart dropped down to the floor. Someone could have knocked her over with a feather. "Absolutely not!" She said, her disapproval resonating in her voice.

"What?" Theodore looked taken aback, as if he had not considered that she would question his offer.

"That is entirely inappropriate!"

"If our family connections were not so close, perhaps…" This time Kelly cut him off.

"If you were a brother-in-law or an uncle, perhaps. But this is absolutely inappropriate!" Kelly began to wring her hands. Lord, this was the height of humiliation.

"No one would need to know the source of your dowry." He said matter-of-factly.

"I would know! My parents would know! They could never accept your...I could never accept your...pity." Her voice dropped from angry to wounded on that last word.

"And yet you would force my hand into a marriage I do not want?" He said without thinking. Kelly stepped back as if from a physical blow. Of course, he didn't want to marry her. If he had, he would have done so by now rather than dragging out their farce of an engagement. But the words still stung, so much more than she had expected.

Seeing the look on Kelly's face, Theodore wished he could call the words back. He wanted to put his arms around Kelly and make the pain on her face go away. He was startled by the thought. It was totally inappropriate. What was coming over him?

Kelly summoned all of her resolve and tried to affect the mask of indifference that Theodore wore so well. "Our marriage is a contractual agreement made by our parents. It is a legally signed document. I am merely asking you to uphold your end of the agreement, as I am ready to do." For the first time in his life, Theo felt the cold burn of Kelly's indifference. From his father, it was expected. For him, it had become a kind of protective armor. But in Kelly, it was altogether different and disconcerting.

Forcing himself to respond in kind, he answered coolly. "Please consider my offer and the benefits it entails. You would be free to choose whomever you like for your husband." He stood and made to leave. "Except for Christopher Bowden."

Chapter 13

*T*wo days later, as she stood at Madison's side at a ball given by the Lord and Lady Westerland, Kelly still mulled over everything that Theodore had said. His offer was very generous, although she could never accept it. It was inappropriate, and if anyone ever found out it would be a scandal of the highest order. There was also her pride and that of her family. Although they had fallen far, she knew in her heart her mother and father would never be able to accept the offer.

She tried to look at the young gentleman arrayed around her in a different light. She had always been betrothed; she had always taken it as a given that Theodore would one day be her husband. As she studied the assembled men, she found that even if given the choice, her thoughts still turned persistently to Theo.

As if knowing that he was in her thoughts, she spotted Theo approaching from across the room. She matched his bow with a ladylike curtsey of greeting.

"Good evening, Miss Collins," He smiled, but Kelly wondered if it was genuine. His every move was always so calculated. She had thought she had seen flashes of emotion, but maybe that was all contrived as well. She honestly did not know. "May I have the honor of the next dance?" He asked.

Kelly glanced at her dance card. "I believe it is already spoken for, my lord." She said.

"Then perhaps a different dance," He caught her card in his hand, consulted it, and then wrote his name. "I will see you soon." He promised, smiling that too perfectly engineered smile again.

"He didn't even say hello to me!" Madison said, a bemused smile on her face. "He really must be smitten with you, Kelly."

"Ha," Kelly laughed sarcastically. Although she hadn't given her new friend the specifics of her situation with Theo, she sensed that Madison had put most of it together on her own, through astute observation and probably some insight from her husband.

"He is different around you, you know," Madison said gently. Kelly gave her a doubtful look. Madison nodded her head. "I've known Theo for several years now. He is always so…controlled. And yet, with you, I think he seems to lose control."

"Is that a good thing?" Kelly asked doubtfully.

"I don't know," Madison shrugged, but then smiled. "But I've certainly never seen him lose control around any other ladies." Kelly mulled over that thought for a while. Since that engaging young boy had disappeared to boarding school and returned a straight-laced young man, Kelly had been keenly aware of the wall of formality that Theodore erected between them. And yet, there had been moments over the past weeks when she had seen it crack: in his outbursts to Christopher Bowden, and most notably in his mysterious kiss. Maybe the boy she had adored was still there, somewhere beneath the surface.

Kelly danced twice more before the dance claimed by Theodore came around. As the first few melodious notes rang out, she began to wonder if he had forgotten her. Then he appeared suddenly, as if out of nowhere.

Theodore forced himself to count to ten before he approached Kelly to claim his dance. He did not want to appear too eager. Taking her in his arms on the dance floor, he couldn't help but notice how well they fit together. From his height, he could see the rich, deep brown color of her hair. She wore it so perfectly bound up now, yet he remembered the long, unrestrained locks she had sported in their youth. He wondered how long her hair was now, if it still curled slightly at the ends. He also had a view of her well-formed breasts, concealed with all propriety by her modest debutante's dress, but whose delectable curve could not be missed from his angle.

"Lord Alston?" Kelly said questioningly. Theodore shook his head as if clearing it. Was he really daydreaming about her breasts? Kelly Collins? He had known her since she was a child! "You're staring," Kelly said when he did not respond.

"I beg your pardon, my lady." He said quickly. Kelly considered him. He had indeed been staring at her, at her breasts, in particular, she suspected. Perhaps he was not as disinterested as he would have her believe. He gave her a charming, clearly contrived smile. "I was considering which of your laudable attributes to focus on while talking to your prospective suitors." He said.

She bit her lip and frowned. "I do not have prospective suitors, remember?"

"Ah, but see, you need to change your perspective. If you accept my offer, you can have your pick of the *ton's* most eligible young men." He nodded his head towards the crowds of noblemen present. "You should begin thinking of all of them as your prospective suitors."

"I will not be accepting your offer." She said firmly, the frown setting more deeply on her pretty face. He had an immediate desire to make it disappear.

"Enough of that. No young man wants a woman who is cross and disagreeable and unhappy."

"I do not care what other young men want!" She said, perhaps a bit too loudly. She earned the glances of other dancers near them. Looking down, she concentrated on her feet as they moved to the rhythmic music.

She felt Theodore's hand gently touch beneath her chin, raising her face to his. "I do not want to see you unhappy." He said softly.

Kelly felt the flood of emotions course through her. Her dark eyes stared up into his bright blue ones. His face moved closer to hers. She held her breath. The air between them was electric, as it had been in Madison's parlor days ago. Had it only been days? It felt like weeks. She knew he was going to kiss her, she was sure of it.

Then the music ended, and he took a step away from her. He pulled her hand to his lips and kissed it, all very proper. She chided herself. Of course, he was not going to kiss her, here in the middle of Lady Westerland's ballroom, in front of half of polite society.

As he led her off of the dance floor, Kelly felt keen disappointment. As they neared where Madison was waiting, she felt his hand leave hers. The tide of disappointment began to flow through her. Then she felt his warm breath in her ear. "Meet me in the garden in ten minutes."

And then he was gone.

He didn't know why he had asked her to meet him. There was no clear purpose; there was nothing he planned to say or do to further his plan. But he had said the words before he could stop himself. And here he was, waiting for her. He rubbed his hand over his face and tried to clear his head. He had to think of some plausible reason for this meeting. There was no way he could let her know that it was his raging desire that had gotten out of control.

She didn't say anything when she arrived. She hung back, watching him for a moment. The Westerland's gardens were extensive and exquisitely maintained. Theo was waiting for her under an arbor twined with vines, and she was partially obscured from his view by a thick hedge. He rubbed his hand up over his face, tousling his hair. She smiled, remembering a younger Theo, one who did not shield his emotions. He was unguarded now, and he looked…worried. She sighed. He was probably worried about the fact that he was having no success getting her to go along with his scheme. Setting the line of her lips firm, she stepped forward to join him.

"Lord Alston," She greeted.

He couldn't stop the smile that came to his face naturally, so he tried to play it off. "Miss Collins, thank you for joining me. I had some thoughts about gentlemen you should consider, but the ballroom didn't seem the most prudent place to continue our conversation." He said smoothly.

Kelly rolled her eyes. "As I've told you, again and again, I'm not considering any other gentleman."

"You think that now, but if you got to know some of them, perhaps developed an affection for one of them, then perhaps you would find it easier to take me up on my offer." He suggested. As he talked, he walked casually through the arbor, toying with a leaf that hung down, feigning a level of disinterest in the whole conversation. Annoyed, Kelly followed him. She planted herself directly in front of him.

Hands on her hips, she said, "I will not go about forming an attachment to someone I cannot marry. First of all, as we are engaged, society would not look at all favorably upon me. And secondly, I do not relish the heartache of developing romantic feelings for someone I cannot have." *Especially because I already have romantic feelings for you*, her mind finished. That set her back. *Oh dear,* she thought. That was an unexpected wrinkle.

"What would you know about romantic feelings?" Theo quirked a brow, his face close to hers. Too close, she had put herself too close. Her mind told her to step back, but her body did not listen. She could not say which part of her psyche directed her next action. She must have lost her mind, because she leaned up, and pressed her lips to his.

Theo opened his mouth in surprise. His reaction was natural, physical, beyond his control, he told himself later. His body leaned closer to hers, his tongue gently nudging her lips apart and deepening the kiss. She made a little sound of surprise, but welcomed him, her lips moving experimentally against his, her body pressing closer to him of its own volition.

She felt that same warmth she felt whenever he touched her. It started at her lips, spread through her chest and body, to previously unknown places, stirring new feelings and desires. She felt the urge to touch him. She reached out with her hands to embrace him.

Her gentle touch was like a spark. Theo broke away from her instantly. He saw the surprise on her face at his withdrawal, and the quick up and down of her chest as she took several deep breaths. He felt his breath coming quick and hot. In a familiar motion, he raked his hand over his face and through his hair. Minutes seemed to pass as they each silently regained their composure.

When he finally trusted himself enough to speak, he said, "I will call on you tomorrow, for a walk in the royal gardens, so we may discuss things further." She turned her eyes up to his, full of questions and emotions. He leaned down and gently kissed her cheek, and then he left before he lost every last vestige of his control.

Chapter 14

*D*rat, drat, drat the man, Kelly thought as she paced anxiously in her parlor. One minute he was calmly telling her she should be considering other suitors, the next he was setting clandestine meetings and kissing her. *Well, she kissed him*, she corrected herself. But it was not as if he had protested.

He did not want to marry her; his insistence on her accepting his offer made that clear enough. But he certainly was not ambivalent to her. She bit her lip as she thought that over.

"You certainly have yourself worked up into a tizzy." Claire Collins observed as she entered the room. Kelly's mother seated herself primly on the sofa and looked up at her daughter expectantly. When she didn't receive an answer, she pressed. "How are things coming along with Lord Alston? I saw you dance together last night; he seemed quite taken with you."

"I doubt that, Mother." Kelly sighed heavily. Her mother didn't know the half of it. She felt sure that Theodore had some feelings towards her, but she couldn't make sense of them herself. Physical desire? Perhaps. A sense of duty? Most likely. Desire to marry her? Nonexistent.

"Nonsense. He couldn't keep his eyes off of you all evening!"

"We only danced once," Kelly said skeptically.

"But did he dance with anyone else?" Claire asked. Kelly didn't know the answer to that, but her mother answered her own question. "No, he did not. He just hovered and watched. He is paying you quite a lot of attention, which is certainly a good thing."

Kelly could see how her mother would think so. "But that does not mean he wants to marry me." She tried to keep the sadness out of her voice.

"No young man wants to get married, Kelly, but he has a duty to fulfill. That is our purpose here, remember? To make sure that he honors that duty." She said. Kelly felt her heart drop. Yes, that was why they had come to London. When had Kelly come to care so much about whether Theo wanted to marry her, instead of simply whether or not he would?

She knew the answer. She had felt this way all along, deep down, because she cared about Theo. She wanted him to be happy. Despite everything that had happened between them in the past, he was her friend. The idea of forcing him to do something that made him unhappy made her heart ache.

But I can make him happy, a small voice inside of her said. The question was: could she convince Theodore of that? She was not a manipulative person; her complete lack of guile and how quickly she had come clean to Theodore about her situation attested to that. But she did believe she could make him happy. She had to find a way to make Theo believe that too.

As if knowing he was in her thoughts, Theo appeared in the doorway, announced by the butler. Claire leaped to her feet. "Lord Alston! What a pleasure to see you again so soon!" She said effusively.

"Lady Collins," He bowed slightly to Claire, but his gaze went almost immediately to Kelly. Though he spoke to Kelly's mother, his eyes were fixed intently on Kelly. "I hoped to take your daughter for an outing to the royal gardens."

"Of course." Kelly's mother glanced nervously between the two of them. She could feel the undercurrent of charged energy between them, but from the look on her face, it was clear that she wasn't sure what to make of it.

Kelly rolled her eyes at her mother's antics. "Augustine?" Kelly called to the butler who was returning to the hall. "Could you please fetch my maid to escort us?" The elderly man nodded and disappeared from the room. Theo extended his arm to Kelly, who moved to take it and allow him to escort her to the carriage outside.

"I will accompany you as well!" Her mother said suddenly. Both Kelly and Theodore turned around abruptly to face her. Kelly knew she wore her surprise on her face; thus far her mother had been completely willing to let Kelly negotiate her relationship with Theodore on her own, even pushing her to be in less than proper situations with Theodore. But apparently, her faith in Kelly's ability to get a commitment from Lord Alston was wavering.

Theodore's face was inscrutable. Kelly wondered what he was thinking, but he gave no clue. He simply nodded and then said respectfully, "Of course, Lady Collins."

Theo kept up the stiff façade throughout the carriage ride. Kelly's mother accompanying them was a wrinkle he hadn't counted on. It would make it considerably more difficult to have an effective conversation with Kelly. He knew she didn't want him to present her mother with his offer to pay for her dowry, and he was going to respect that wish. Besides, Kelly was the one he needed to convince. Once she gave in to the logic of his plan, he was confident that her parents would go along with it simply to please her. Their adoration and love for their only child had always been obvious.

Claire tried several times to start conversations, but Theo was so deeply caught up in his musings that all of her attempts fell flat.

"It seems an eternity since we've seen you out at Middleborough Manor, Lord Alston. We would be most excited to receive you sometime soon." Kelly's mother said with a smile, her words fraught with implications.

"Indeed," Theo said noncommittally. Sitting across from him, Kelly shot him a reproving glance in response to his clipped reply. She saw him smile slightly at her, then direct his attention fixedly out the window. She looked down at her hands, trying to calm her quickened pulse from their silently shared exchange.

Finally, they arrived. Theo alighted from the carriage, turning back to hand down Claire and then Kelly. Putting her hand in Theo's, Kelly allowed him to help her down. When he moved to let go, she held on for a moment, giving his hand a quick squeeze. Theodore glanced down at her and was met with her small, shy smile. He seemed to think for a moment, then he tucked her hand into his arm companionably and led her up the path. Kelly's mother was talking about something regarding the gardens, but Kelly didn't hear a word she said.

They moved as a group through the gardens for a few minutes, without having much of a conversation. The flowers were in bloom and it was a lovely setting, romantic by anyone's standards. Kelly wondered why Theo had chosen to bring her here. It was the sort of thing a man who was courting would do to try and impress the young woman he was seeking. Since that clearly couldn't be the case, she wondered at his motivations.

They reached a fork in the path, and Theodore took the opportunity to speak up. "Lady Collins, I would like to show Miss Collins a particularly rare flower just over this way. Would you permit me to…?" He trailed off, but his suggestion was clear. Would he be allowed to have a few moments of privacy with Kelly?

"Of course!" Claire said quickly, loath the deny him anything. In her mind, there was very little she would refuse him if it had even the slightest chance of leading to the desired ends. However, she did hesitate for a moment before adding: "You'll of course stay near enough that I can see you? While you are engaged, it wouldn't do to cast any suspicion on Kelly's good name."

"Without a doubt, my lady," Giving a little bow, Theodore didn't wait for a response before leading

Kelly away. He didn't want to give her time to second guess. He needed time to speak to Kelly without her mother hearing their every word.

Kelly couldn't contain her chuckle. "That was not well done, Theo. She is trying so hard to make you happy. She could hardly say 'no'."

"Why is she concerned about making me happy?" Theo asked, clearly confused.

Kelly stopped laughing and sighed. "She thinks if she does anything to offend you, then you won't honor the engagement."

"I see," was all he said in response. Kelly's brow furrowed as she considered him.

"Why are you so set against marrying me, Theo?" Her forthrightness made Theo raise his own eyebrows. Though, he should have expected it by this point. She had been unfailingly honest with him about her reasons for coming to London and for wanting to get married.

"That does not matter, Kelly." He said firmly.

"Of course it does." She said quietly. "We have been betrothed for most of our lives. It never seemed to bother you when we were growing up. So why does it bother you now?" She was making herself vulnerable by asking the question. He could say anything; perhaps he did not find her attractive, or he was in love with someone else. But if Kelly was going to convince him to marry her, she needed whatever insight she could get.

"It doesn't matter." He repeated, though this time Kelly thought she detected a hint of sadness in his voice. She fought the urge to push him further, sensing that he would close up on her if she did. They walked for a few minutes in silence before he spoke again. "The reason I brought you here is to advise you on some gentleman that I think would be worth your consideration."

Kelly's eyebrows shot to the sky. "I thought we had established that was not a viable course of action."

He ignored her. "Lord Allan Towton would be an acceptable match. He isn't overly wealthy, but his family is titled and the estates are prosperous enough that incorporating Middleborough wouldn't be too much trouble. Harry Brandt, Earl of Northrup is well-liked by men and women alike, and an avid horseman. You always liked riding well enough."

"This is ridiculous…"

"Evan Eislander is not titled but is extremely wealthy. His family is new money, but you don't seem the type to judge someone because of that." He continued, ignoring Kelly's protestations.

Kelly felt her temper rising. So, this was why he had brought her here: to try and browbeat her into accepting his offer and choosing a new fiancé. "Well how about Christopher Bowden? He is from a good family, and he has already expressed his interest." She countered, hands going to her hips automatically.

"I've already told you, he is not an option." He said shortly, trying not to let himself take the bait that her combative stance and tone of voice offered.

"Who are you to say who is and who is not an option?" She said angrily.

"I do not like the way he looks at…"

This time, Kelly interrupted him as they rounded the corner of the path, putting them momentarily out of the view of her mother. "Why do you care?"

"Because I care about you!" He almost shouted.

Theodore froze. What was it about her that made him lose control, every time? *He cared about her?* Of course, he did; she was his childhood companion and friend. It was nothing more than that, he told himself stubbornly.

He had brought her here because he knew she missed the countryside, and he thought the gardens might make her happy. If she was happy, she would be more amenable to his plans and might agree to go along with him. That was what he told himself, at least.

Kelly laughed. "You don't need to act so surprised, Theodore. Even you can feel emotions." She said. He looked at her in confusion. Why had her anger been so suddenly replaced by mirth?

Kelly felt like she was glowing. *Because I care about you.* She heard his words echo in her head as she turned to face him fully. "I care about you too." She said softly.

"Oh lord," she thought she heard him mutter before his lips met hers. This time, he didn't hesitate to invade her sweet, unpracticed mouth. He claimed it instantly, as if it was his to explore and enjoy. His hands cupped her soft cheeks and held her in place, so she couldn't retreat.

Retreat was the farthest thing from her mind. Kelly felt like she was being carried away on a cloud to her own personal heaven. Her glimpse into his feelings, however fleeting, had given her hope.

Hearing her mother's voice and step coming nearer, Theo broke away. It was their briefest kiss yet, as they knew her mother would appear around the corner at any moment. But to Kelly, it felt the most special.

Chapter 15

As he slowed his horse to a walk, Theodore was thankful for the brief respite that the physical exertion had given him. For days, he had been trying very hard not to think about Kelly Collins. And he had been failing miserably. At least for the few minutes he and Henry were galloping along, his focus had been on his mount. Pulling his horse up alongside his friend, Henry seemed to read his mind.

"How is your engagement developing?" He asked, a mischievous glint in his eye.

Theodore gave his horse a solid kick and trotted ahead of his friend in response. He heard Henry's laughter over his shoulder as his friend kicked his mount to catch up.

Unfazed by Theo's attempts at evasion, Henry said "Madison said you took her to the royal gardens the day before yesterday."

"And if I did?" Theo said sharply. He did not want to have this conversation.

"Seems like a real courtship you are carrying on." His friend observed, undeterred by Theo's tone of voice.

"We are engaged, as you seem to enjoy pointing out. It is hardly inappropriate to walk around some plants with one's fiancée."

"True enough," Henry nodded as they rounded the corner of the street where Henry and Madison's townhouse was located. Thankful that the topic had finally been dropped, Theodore was about to ask Henry about his newly purchased horse when his friend interrupted him. "But for someone who isn't planning on marrying the girl, you seem to be spending a lot of time with her."

Theo sighed heavily as they arrived and dismounted, handing over their horses to be stabled. "We have known one another for a long time. We are friends."

"It seems like a lot more than friendship to me," Henry observed as they climbed the stairs and entered the house. "I've seen the way you look at her. If I wasn't completely in love with my wife, I would give her more than a second look." He winked suggestively. "And you have to have noticed that other gentlemen are already doing as much."

"She's my fiancée," Theodore said with finality, as if that brooked no further discussion. But Henry would not be stymied.

"But what does that mean? If you refuse to marry the girl, then stop wasting her time and let her get on with her life."

"I'm not wasting her time, I'm helping her."

"Helping her do what?"

"Find a suitable husband."

"From what I can tell, you are the husband she wants."

"I…" Theo started to respond but was cut short as Madison walked into the entryway, cutting off the men's retreat to Henry's study.

"Good morning, love," Henry kissed his wife's cheek. She embraced him, but her eyes never left Theo.

"Henry, I'd like a private word with Theodore." She said. Her voice was even and calm, but the glint in her eyes made Theo's warning bells go off. He looked quickly to his friend, who put his hands up in surrender. He would not intercede with his wife. Giving him a mock salute, Henry ducked past Madison and continued down the hallway to his study. "The parlor, if you please." She said to Theo, motioning towards the open door.

Theo moved into the room, declining to sit and instead taking a place leaning against the wall, his arms crossed in front of his body. "What is it, Madison?" He asked directly.

She answered him with matching directness. "What are you going to do about Kelly?"

Unshaken, he raised his eyebrows at her. "What concern is it of yours?"

"She is my friend."

"She is my friend as well." He countered.

"She cares for you very much." She said, her lips pursed.

"I care for her as well." He said honestly.

Madison shook her head, not accepting his answer. "She cares for you in a romantic sense. She wants to marry you."

"She doesn't know what she wants. She has this idea in her head that we must marry, and she cannot let it go." He truly believed that. If she would get over her pride, and accept his offer, she would see that there were many gentlemen better suited to her than he was.

"You underestimate her," Madison responded.

"What do you mean by that?" He asked, truly wondering at her answer. What did she mean by that?

"Her feelings are deeply involved in this, much more than I think you realize. I do not want to see her get hurt." She said, emotion in her voice. Though they had known each other only a short time, Madison had become very attached to Kelly. And if Madison cared about someone, she loved them with her whole heart and would protect them fiercely. Theo knew this; but what he wondered was, why would Madison think that Kelly needed to be protected from him?

"I have been protecting her since we were children. Do you think I would hurt her?" He felt his ire rising, and his calm façade slipping. It was ridiculous, the idea that he would hurt Kelly. That was a large part of the reason he did not want to marry her: their marriage would inevitably devolve into bitterness and resentment, and he did not want to be responsible for inflicting that kind of pain on Kelly. Madison could not be more wrong, he thought to himself.

"Not intentionally," Madison answered. "But I think you are so determined not to get married, that you don't see what is right in front of you."

"Which is?" He said icily, offended by Madison's disregard.

He saw Madison force herself to take a couple of deep breaths, and then she responded calmly. "Not all marriages are unhappy, Theodore. Look at Henry and me." She sighed deeply. "You are my friend as well, Theo. All I am asking is that you think about how you truly feel, and what you truly want, because whether you intended it or not, both of your feelings are now involved."

"My feelings…" He started to protest but she shook her head to silence him. She leaned up, gave him a kiss on the cheek, and left him to try and figure out what the hell it all meant.

Chapter 16

"What do you think of the blue one? Do you think it compliments my eyes?" Madison asked, tilting the peacock blue hat upon her head to a very fashionable angle while carefully observing the effect in the nearby looking-glass.

Kelly gave her a doubtful look, eliciting a loud laugh from her friend.

"You don't even need to say how ridiculous you think it is; your eyes tell all." Madison chuckled, replacing the hat on its velveteen stand. "Ah, but that one over there…" She trailed off as she wandered to the other side of the shop.

Kelly rolled her eyes and sighed, following behind her friend half-heartedly. They had been in this shop for nearly half an hour. And had lingered in the bookshop and the jewelry shop before that. She was bored to tears; shopping was not her cup of tea. She preferred to be outside, and walking around stuffy shops deciding how to fritter away money was not her idea of an afternoon well spent. Honestly, she did not know what Madison was doing here either. She hadn't ever seen Madison in a hat, and certainly not in anything so garish. And yet here she was dallying and insisting on trying on every item in the shop.

She heard the jingle of the bell that hung over the shop's door, announcing another patron. Kelly glanced over her shoulder to observe the pair that entered: a petite, blonde young woman who did not look a day over seventeen, accompanied by a tall, quite handsome blonde man. Finding nothing of particular interest, Kelly turned her attention back towards locating Madison. But before she could do so, her friend rushed up to greet the newly arrived pair.

"Arianna! What a pleasure to see you!" Madison greeted the young woman with a wide smile, taking her hand in her own familiarly. Kelly could see that the girl seemed a little uneasy. She smiled inwardly to herself; Madison's gregarious manner could be a little intimidating until you got used to it. "Kelly, do come here and meet Arianna!"

Amused at Madison's unabashed friendliness, Kelly joined them and offered a polite smile.

"Arianna Eislander, this is Miss Kelly Collins, of Middleborough. Kelly, this is Arianna Eislander, and her brother, Evan Eislander." Madison made the introductions. Why did their names sound familiar? Kelly asked herself. She looked at them again, closer this time, to determine if she may have met them before. However, she couldn't place them.

Arianna seemed too overwhelmed to speak, but she smiled nervously. Seeing her up close, it was apparent that she was young, maybe only fifteen or so. She certainly wasn't "out" in society yet; she would perhaps make her *ton* debut in a year or two. Kelly returned her smile, empathizing with the younger woman's shy awkwardness.

"Our families are both from Devonshire," Madison explained. "But Arianna and Evan have only recently come to town."

"I am new to town as well, Miss Eislander, Lord Eislander. How do you like it here?" Kelly asked kindly, thinking she now could understand Arianna's shyness. London was a lot to take in, especially for a young woman raised in the quiet countryside.

"Ah, it's just Mr. Eislander, actually," the brother, Evan, corrected with a small smile. "We are adjusting; it is quite different than country life."

That's where she recognized the name! *Not titled, but extremely wealthy*, was how Theodore had described Evan Eislander as a potential suitor. Kelly suppressed the urge to roll her eyes; as if she cared about such petty things. Thankful that she indeed hadn't met them before and simply forgotten them, which would have been quite embarrassing, she turned her attention back to Miss Eislander. "Yes, I miss my home very much. It is difficult to be in a new city where you do not know many people." She smiled sympathetically, and she thought she saw some of the tension in Arianna's shoulders ease.

"Arianna has not made her come out yet, so she hasn't had a chance to meet anyone here," Evan explained, putting a protective arm around his sister's shoulders.

"But she is to have her come out soon, yes? The Season has just begun." Madison asked.

"Yes, but not until next Season." Evan confirmed.

"I would be happy to help make introductions in the meantime," Madison said kindly. "I know of many families who have daughters of similar age. She would be able to socialize and get to know some of them before her debut. It is so helpful to have friendly faces around you when you are presented to society for the first time."

"That is very kind, Lady Warsham, my sister and I would greatly appreciate it," he replied. He turned his eyes to Kelly, his interest in her evident. "Where in the country are you from?" He asked warmly. Kelly felt herself blush.

Before Kelly could answer, the bell rang again. Out of habit, Kelly threw a cursory glance over her shoulder. But she immediately did a double-take when she recognized the woman that had entered the shop.

"Lady Alston," She sank into a deep curtsey automatically. Every time she had met Theodore's mother, she had been instructed to be on her very best behavior. It had been so long since she had seen the older lady; since Theodore's father's funeral, she believed. Lady Alston looked mostly unchanged; she was attractive still, her iron-gray hair styled fashionably and sharply dressed in deep burgundy. She radiated an aura of stately elegance. But Kelly knew that she herself had changed. She had been a child then; now she was a woman, both in appearance and maturity. What would Theodore's mother think of her now?

"Good afternoon, Miss Collins," Lady Alston said amiably. She looked Kelly up and down, and Kelly very much got the feeling of an item being appraised at auction. Fortunately, she seemed to be found passable for Lady Alston fixed her gaze back on Kelly's face and smiled. "You have certainly grown up nicely, my dear."

"Thank you," Kelly managed to say, trying very hard not to mumble. Theodore's mother seemed pleased with her, at least initially. That was a relief.

"Lady Alston, I am so pleased to see you again!" Madison exclaimed, smiling widely. She turned to the other two young people with them. "Mr. Eislander, Miss Eislander, this is Lady Alston, Countess of Willingham. Her son, Lord Alston, is a dear friend."

"A pleasure to meet you, my lady," Evan Eislander bowed and his sister dropped into a proper curtsey. "I do not think that we have met at any events this season. Have you just come up to town?"

"Indeed, I've come to assist my son in planning his upcoming nuptials. Ah, here he is…" She turned as the door opened behind her and Theodore walked unsuspectingly into the quickly crowding shop. "Theodore, I've come upon Lady Warsham and Miss Collins and their friends most unexpectedly!" She proclaimed. Theodore's eyes narrowed. He glanced from his mother to Madison, feeling sure there was nothing 'unexpected' about this meeting.

This was clearly part of the scheme that his mother and Madison had been concocting when he had happened upon them having tea together. He also had no doubt as to their intentions; they were of a single mind with regards to him and Kelly. Somehow, this supposed chance meeting was meant to advance his relationship with Kelly.

"Eislander," he said with a nod. He had met Evan Eislander on several occasions. They were members of the same gentleman's club. He did not know him well, but he had a reputation as a shrewd businessman and generally affable person. Overall, he seemed harmless. Which was why he had proposed him as a potential suitor for Kelly. However, seeing them standing together, with Evan's eyes smiling enthusiastically at Kelly and a very becoming blush on Kelly's cheeks, he found that he did not like the man much at all. "Madison, Miss Collins." He acknowledged Kelly with the slightest inclination of his head. But his eyes held hers for one paralyzing moment before darting back to his mother.

"Congratulations, Lord Alston, we've just been informed of your upcoming marriage." Evan Eislander said. Theodore's eyes flew accusingly to Kelly, but before she could defend herself his mother stepped in.

"As I said, we have many details still to settle." Eleanor supplied in response. She turned deliberately towards Kelly. "Miss Collins, I would be most obliged if you would call upon me tomorrow so that we may begin discussing details."

The implication was clear and not missed by Mr. Eislander. "Miss Collins is your bride, then?" Evan's eyebrows rose.

Theodore shot him a dark look. He did not like the warm appreciation that filled Eislander's eyes as he had looked at Kelly. Everywhere she went the woman had men falling at her feet. It was damnably annoying. And why did it bother him so damn much? That was a question he was determined not to explore further.

"I would be happy to call on you, Lady Alston," Kelly replied, saving Theodore from saying something he most certainly would have regretted. Theo was very good at masking his emotions, but she had seen enough of his interactions with Christopher Bowden to suspect that there was something less than favorable brewing beneath his carefully calm exterior.

"Excellent, I am looking forward to it." Eleanor turned back to her son. "Theodore, this was not the shop I wanted after all. Please escort me outside so we may get about our business." His mother had accomplished what she wanted: a pretext for meeting Kelly and making their marriage seem as if it was already a foregone conclusion. He would have to talk to his mother about this; he could not allow this to go on. However, this was not the venue.

"Of course," He answered instead. Taking his mother's arm, Theo bid goodbye to the other members of the party. When his eyes landed on Kelly, they were indiscernible. "Until tomorrow, it would seem." He said softly.

Chapter 17

"Where are you off to, Theodore?" His mother's voice called from the sitting room. He nodded to his butler to give directions to have his horse saddled and then turned back to answer his mother. After they left Bond Street the previous afternoon, he had quickly deposited his mother back at the townhouse and made excuses about having previous commitments for the evening. In reality, he had retreated to his gentleman's club to avoid his mother's sidelong glances and too-knowing looks. He knew that he needed to speak with her and tell her firmly that his engagement to Kelly was not going forward. But she was still his mother, and contradicting her was never easy. When she took breakfast in her room this morning, he thought for sure he was in the clear.

Lady Eleanor was perched on the sofa, drinking tea and looking serene. "Good morning, Mother. I am off to join Henry Warsham. We have a few parliamentary matters to discuss."

"Surely Henry can wait a few minutes. Miss Collins will be arriving shortly and I would like you to be here to greet her." His mother said nonchalantly, as if having tea with his fiancée was a completely normal occurrence.

Theo gritted his teeth. There was no avoiding the conversation now, he supposed, resigning himself to the task. "Mother, that is not a good idea."

"Don't you like Miss Collins?"

"Of course I do."

"Don't you find her pleasant? Enjoyable to talk to? Attractive?"

I find her far too pleasant and attractive for my own good, he thought to himself. But he carefully replied to his mother without emotion. "We have already discussed my views on Miss Collins. They have not changed."

"Theodore, I have invited her here to discuss the details of your upcoming wedding, and it would not be at all polite if you are not at least here to say hello." His mother said firmly, putting down her teacup and giving him a resolute stare.

"It is unfair of you to invite her here under such pretenses. I have made it quite clear to Miss Collins that there will be no wedding." He said bluntly.

Eleanor made a dismissive gesture, appearing unfazed by his protestations. "Then she is here so that we may become reacquainted. I have known her since she was a girl and I want to better know the young woman she has become. Tell me, Theodore, what is she like?"

Perfect. That was the first word that jumped into Theo's mind. *Perfect curves, perfect lips, the perfect way of making him smile and laugh without even seeming to try.*

"She's very well mannered." He said instead, trying to suppress the other thoughts.

His mother scoffed. "That's all you have to say?"

Totally engrossing, "She's pleasant enough to have a conversation with." He stated.

Eleanor rolled her eyes. "Well, I suppose I will have to find out for myself since you are quite useless." She countered, pouring herself another cup of tea. Theo didn't respond. He could sense that this game he was playing was becoming dangerous. He was far too aware of Kelly's virtues.

His objection to marriage to Kelly was philosophical, not personal. It wasn't that he didn't want to marry her, exactly, it was that he didn't want to *be* married at all. His parent's marriage had been a disaster. For all the world, theirs had been a perfectly content and exemplary family. His father managed the estate and his lordly duties, his mother oversaw the house and her wifely role with aplomb, and he rounded out the picture as the well-spoken and attentive son. The reality had been much more untenable.

His parents' relationship had been cold and emotionless. The elder Lord Alston regarded his son with that same degree of affection. For many years, Theodore had watched his mother buckle under his father's cold edicts. He had felt the brunt of his father's cruel barbs, and occasionally the back of his hand. And Theo saw himself as the mirror of his father, physically and emotionally.

His parents' marriage had been a painful disaster for everyone involved. Theodore had no intention of putting himself in such a position, for the rest of his life. No matter how enticing Kelly Collins was, he was certain that eventually, they would devolve into the same unhappiness. It was a state he intended to avoid as long as possible. He was gearing up to tell his mother something of the sort when they were interrupted.

"My lady, Miss Collins has arrived." The Alston's butler appeared in the doorway, bringing Theo out of his reverie. Theo made a disgruntled noise; despite his protestations, his mother had managed to get exactly what she wanted. Her superior smile grated on him as she instructed the servant to show Miss Collins into the room to join them.

Kelly entered the room with a smile, which he thought deepened when her eyes landed on him. He felt his smile lighting naturally in response, and he inwardly cursed, reminding himself that he needed to keep better control of himself around her. She was a vision in her rose-colored gown. The color accented her cheeks, and the scooped neckline of the gown immediately had him thinking about her breasts, wondering if the pink of her dress matched the pink of her...

"Miss Collins, it is so lovely to see you. Thank you for joining me on such short notice." Lady Eleanor said, greeting Kelly warmly. She motioned to the sofa where she was seated, inviting Kelly to join her.

"I am honored at the invitation," Kelly responded politely. She turned her eyes questioningly to Theo. "Lord Alston, I did not expect to see you here today." There was a challenge in her eyes; she knew that he could not further his attempts to dissuade her while his mother looked on. But her eyes dared him to brave the tempest anyways.

His mother jumped in before he could respond. "I asked him to be here with us as well because I have a very important matter to discuss with the two of you."

"Mother," The warning in Theodore's voice when he interrupted her was clear. But she ignored him and continued.

"Since I am so seldom in town, it seemed only appropriate that we host a ball while I am here." She pronounced. Both Theo and Kelly were completely surprised. They had not expected that at all. Unfazed by their silence, Eleanor continued. "While I am not often in town anymore, I am still considered an important societal matron, and so we can be assured that it will be well attended."

Kelly doubted that any ball given at the residence of the Earl of Willingham would be anything but well attended. She understood the Countess's desire to host an event; since Lady Eleanor preferred the country, much as Kelly did, she did not have many such opportunities to socialize with the larger sphere of the *ton*. What she did not understand, however, was why Lady Eleanor had requested her presence for this meeting.

"Mother, this is unnecessary. There are many other balls you can attend to socialize with your friends; we needn't invite the crush right through the front door." Theo protested predictably. He didn't like attending *ton* social events, much less hosting them in his own home. As a bachelor, he was spared the headache.

"On the contrary, Theodore, it is completely necessary. It will be my last bow as the Countess of Willingham before I become the dowager. It will be a passing of the baton, of sorts." Eleanor turned her eyes to Kelly. "Miss Collins, I would deeply appreciate your assistance in the planning and execution. It is the perfect way to cement your new position within the *ton*."

Kelly could see Theodore's frustration rising. He was not handling his mother's blindsiding him particularly well. She felt torn; Theo's mother was being exceptionally kind to her. Eleanor was giving her an entre into the elite world of the ton, making sure that society knew that she approved of her and her marriage to her son. However, Kelly knew exactly how Theodore felt about that. Kelly's mission when she came to London had been to ensure that Theodore married her and ensure that her family avoided financial ruin. Now that his mother was here, ready to assist her in all but forcing his hand, she couldn't help but feel like she was betraying Theo.

But in the end, she caved to the combined familial pressures.

"I would be happy to assist you in any way I can." Kelly forced herself to say. She saw Theodore's countenance darken and close up. She knew that he wanted her to refuse, but she couldn't do it. Planning with Lady Alston would require many meetings and therefore opportunities for Kelly to interact with Theo, and try to convince him that she could make him happy as his wife.

"Excellent! We should start planning out the guest list immediately." Eleanor took her victory as her due, smiling triumphantly. "You may go about your parliamentary business now, Theodore. We will relay the important particulars to you in due course." She said, dismissing him and turning back to Kelly.

Theodore barely succeeded in keeping his frustration in check. He said a curt goodbye and left while he still maintained some modicum of control. His mother had openly defied his wishes regarding advancing his relationship with Kelly. And Kelly had gone right along with her. He had been effectively outmaneuvered. Which left him wondering how on earth he was going to convince Kelly to give up her notions of marriage, when everyone but him seemed to be on her side.

Chapter 18

Kelly met with Lady Alston several times over the next two weeks to plan the Countess' celebration. Lady Alston had even called upon Kelly's mother; and although they did not explicitly speak of marriage, their conversations were stilted with layers of meaning that neither one attempted to disguise. Their mothers seemed to be steaming steadily forward with the notion that their marriage was imminent, despite Kelly's continued protests to her mother that nothing Theodore had said or done indicated that he was any closer to accepting their union. For his part, Kelly was sure that Theodore had told his mother much the same.

Theodore had studiously avoided her since that morning in his parlor with his mother. Although she had visited his townhouse many times to meet with Lady Alston, Theodore was conspicuously absent. Even Lady Alston made an offhand comment about her "stubborn son" which in the moment made Kelly chuckle, but in retrospect made her more worried. If his mother was unable to sway him, surely she didn't stand a chance.

With the impending Alston ball scheduled one week hence, Kelly felt a need to escape. Lady Alston, though sweet and kind, had kept her very busy with preparations. When she wasn't attending to details for the upcoming event, her mother was obsessing over what dress and jewelry Kelly should wear or pressing her for information regarding Theo.

Wanting only to be alone, she told her mother she was going for a visit with Madison. By doing so, she knew her mother would not require her to take a maid to escort her; she need only take a footman to drive the carriage. However, after they were a few streets away from her family's residence, Kelly rapped on the roof of the carriage to get the footman's attention.

"Randall, I've remembered that Lady Warsham is not available this afternoon; she told me but I forgot until just now." She tried to sound genuine as the lie left her lips. Guile was not her forte; she usually wore her emotions too close to the surface for her to be convincing. But Randall didn't know her that well, and she was in the carriage while he was outside.

"That is no problem, my lady. I will return you home." He said politely.

"No, please," She said, continuing boldly with the plan she had formulated in her head. "It would be a shame to waste this fine weather, especially since we are already about. If you'll just drive on to the park, and go around by the lake, I'd like to take a walk."

The footman looked uneasy. "We really should return and get a maid or Lady Collins; don't you think my lady?"

"It's just a quick turn around the park. It will be fine, perfectly fine." She tried to sound nonchalant and also firm. She leaned back inside the carriage, hoping that he wouldn't protest. The young Randall seemed to think for a moment, and then the carriage lurched into motion without further protest. It was not long before the carriage came to a stop, and from her glance outside, Kelly confirmed that they had reached the park. She allowed Randall to help her from the carriage but rebuked his desire to walk with her. All she wanted was a few moments of peace. Assuring him that she would stay close and offering him a reassuring smile, she set off for the edge of the lake in the afternoon sunlight.

She walked slowly, first down to the lake and then along the shore into a copse of trees. It was blissfully quiet, just as she had hoped. This area of the park wasn't frequented by her ever-growing number of *ton* acquaintances, so she was left in peace. Closing her eyes, she breathed in the weedy smell of the water, the crisp scent of the grass, the sweet aroma of the wildflowers. Then she smelled something headier. "How did you know I was here?" She asked without turning around.

Theodore paused a few steps behind her. He had approached silently, stopped himself from calling out to her when he saw the way she was reveling in the stillness. "I was coming to call on you. I saw you leave in the carriage and I followed."

Kelly didn't respond immediately. Instead, she sat down on the ground, settling herself in the grass among the flowers. This was a different Kelly; quiet, pensive, reflective. As a youth she had been chatty and gregarious; as a young woman, he had experienced both her wit and her temper. But this was a new side, quietly contemplative. Theodore felt his chest tighten with some unrecognizable feeling.

Dropping down beside her on the ground, he didn't break the silence. He stared out at the lake before them, thinking silently. He had forced himself to stay away from her. She exerted some sort of pull on him that he just couldn't control, and when she was near his good judgment, his years of carefully crafted detachment and cool composure, melted away. And he did not know how to deal with that. So, he had stayed away from her, for two long and agonizing weeks, hoping that the feeling would lessen and he would be able to engage with her like any other young woman of his acquaintance.

She looked like a painting, posed with the sun streaming through her hair and the trees blowing in the breeze behind her. As he looked at her, he feared the separation hadn't mattered at all.

Kelly carefully regarded the man sitting next to her. She tried to reconcile the boy she had known in her childhood, with the stone-faced young man of her adolescence, with the charming, overwhelmingly attractive, but carefully distant man she had come to know in the past month.

Finally, she spoke: "Do you recall that lake we found in the woods on the edge of Middleborough? I must have been nine or ten years old."

Theodore smiled slightly. "I remember. We gave our nurses the slip and pretended to be bandits in the woods."

"I thought that lake was a magical place; it was perfect, undiscovered, it belonged only to us." She said, the image vivid in her mind. "But it wasn't a lake. I went looking for it, a few years later. It's just a big pond. It seemed so different to me, so different than how I remembered it. I was so disappointed. I felt like the world had betrayed me somehow, by not living up to what I expected."

Theo considered for a few moments before responding. "The lake didn't change. But the way you saw it did. Your perspective was different. Your youthful idealism had faded." He replied. He had the feeling they were discussing much more than just a childhood memory.

"Perhaps;" She paused before saying softly "I wonder what I would think of it now."

Unable to come up with a reply, Theo stared out at the lake before them now. The silence stretched between them, neither of them eager to talk about the issues and feelings that presently enveloped them. Eventually, Kelly broke the silence.

"Your mother thinks that I should arrive before the ball starts, so that I may stand with you to greet the guests as they arrive." She said, keeping her eyes carefully trained ahead. Theodore nodded silently. Unable to keep her emotions from bubbling over, Kelly reached for his hand as she continued earnestly. "I want you to know that I've done nothing to encourage or mislead her with regards to your feelings. It is she who insists that we proceed as if a wedding is imminent." Although a wedding to him was what she desperately wanted, it was important to Kelly that he knew she was not trying to deceive him or get to him through his mother. Aside from familial obligations and societal pressures, Kelly found herself most concerned about his feelings.

"I know," he responded. He stared down at her hand closed around his, trying to get a handle on his feelings. He wanted so badly to take her in his arms and erase the confusion and melancholy that she was feeling. He wanted to pull her against him and kiss her full, pink lips that even now were trembling with emotion. He wanted...her.

Theo leaned in towards her, intending to give her a quick embrace, a small show of platonic reassurance. He honestly believed he could do it. But weeks of barely contained desire came straight to the surface, and when he leaned closer and took her lips, there was nothing platonic or innocent about it. The situation they found themselves in might be complicated, his feelings for her were certainly more than he was willing to explore or acknowledge, but this was simple. He was unquestionably attracted to her, and giving in to those physical feelings was easier than contemplating the more complex ones.

Kelly wasn't surprised when he kissed her; on some level, she had expected it from the moment he approached her. The magnetism between them was irresistible. He kissed her softly at first, his lips touching hers lightly, slanting against hers this way and then that. Then he deepened the kiss, sliding his tongue first along the line of her lips, then deeper into her mouth. She felt herself quiver in response as his tongue met hers. Slowly, sweetly, his tongue teased hers, showing her what to do. This time when she reached to touch him, he did not recoil.

As her hands slid up his arms and over his shoulders, his hand slid behind her back and lowered her into the soft grass. Their bodies pressed against each other instinctively, reaching for the closeness they both craved. As they kissed, his hand slid over the front of her gown, to her stomach, and then slowly upward. Kelly was surprised when she felt his hand softly caress the swell of her breast above the neckline of her dress, but the warmth of his touch made her entire body tingle. She clung to him, letting herself kiss him with more ardor and less restraint. She moaned softly when he pulled away.

Theo caressed the tops of her breasts with his knuckles softly, then lowered his lips to her skin. He placed a row of soft kisses along the line where her beautiful breasts disappeared beneath the fabric of her dress. He deftly loosened the front of her gown and slid his hand inside. Kelly gasped as his hand made contact with the tender skin of her breast. He met her gasp with a kiss, steady and intoxicating as his hand began to explore, stroking the smooth skin along the side of her breast and then lightly teasing her nipple until it firmed under his touch. She moaned into him as he kissed her, her body arching against his in primal need and desire that didn't need to be taught.

Then something was calling her back, pulling her from her heady trance. As if through earmuffs, she heard the call: "My lady? Miss Collins?"

Theo heard it too; he pulled himself away from her, looking in the direction of the caller. The small stand of trees partially secluded them from view; that and the distance which Kelly had wandered from the carriage had served as protection to hide them.

"Miss Collins?" the footman called again, clearly getting closer.

Somehow Kelly managed to find her voice. "I'll be right along!" She called, "I'm perfectly fine, please go back to the carriage and ready the horses, I'll be right along." Kelly hoped she sounded more 'perfectly fine' than she felt. She must have convinced Randall, for she heard him retreating in the direction he had come. She let out a sigh of relief. Only then did she look at Theodore.

"Kelly, I shouldn't have…" he started, but she shook her head to stop him.

"You don't need to apologize, Theo." She said. He searched her eyes, looking for anger or guile, but he found none. He helped her straighten her clothes, and then took her hand and drew her to her feet. Squeezing her hands together uneasily, she said "I will see you at the ball."

Theo's eyes held hers for a few moments longer, and then she turned and walked away. *I can't wait*, he heard his heart say quietly.

Chapter 19

"*I*'m not sure about that, let's try it the other way again, pinned back more off of her face," Claire directed the maid standing at Kelly's shoulder, pins sticking out of her mouth where she had put them absently while rearranging Kelly's hair for the fourth or fifth time. Kelly had lost count. She sighed, waving away the compliant maid's hands as she attempted to start again.

"Really mother, it's fine," Kelly said with exasperation.

"Fine is not what we want, Kelly, not in a moment like this," Kelly's mother ushered the maid forward again. "Everything needs to be perfect; tonight is critical to convincing Lord Alston…"

"Convincing him to marry me? And you think after these last two months, my hairstyle is going to do that?" Kelly snapped. She saw her mother's façade falter, but she found she didn't have the energy at the moment to hold together anyone but herself. She had been poked and prodded, fought off her mother's attempts at garish rouge, and endured an ongoing succession of elaborate and ridiculous updos. "I can finish up myself. I will meet you downstairs in a few moments."

"I really do think…" Claire began, but when she saw Kelly's look sharpen she nodded and silently departed, taking the maid with her.

It wasn't until she heard the door click and the sounds of their retreating footsteps down the hall died away to silence that Kelly slowly let out her breath. All she wanted was a few moments of peace to gather her thoughts before descending into the tempest of this evening. In a few minutes, she would have to go downstairs, enter the carriage, and ride the short distance to Theo's residence. Then, before all the notable members of London's *haute ton*, she would stand between Theodore and Eleanor, and preside over this grand event as if she were on the precipice of stepping into that role permanently. Societal matron, countess, wife…

She felt like she was on a precipice alright, but of what she wasn't sure. She felt certain that the next step she and Theo took would be a decisive one. Marriage, happiness, that all-encompassing giddiness she felt when he was near…or loss, humiliation, and betrayal. She turned the words over in her mind, scoffing at how melodramatic they sounded. But even as she did, she realized how true they would be. Until Theodore had reentered her life, she had been sweetly oblivious to the notion that she might need him in it. Now that she had spent time with him again, she remembered. He filled the special place inside her that he had occupied in their youth and then some.

She did not think she would ever be able to forget that or be anything but keenly aware of its loss.

After the way they had carried on, both publicly and privately, she knew the sting of his loss would also cause her deep humiliation. Both from being publically cast aside, and perhaps more painfully, for having naively let their physical relationship advance so far when the outcome was far from assured.

So much hung in the balance. This wasn't just a matter of saving her family and home from ruin anymore. It was about saving herself, and Theo. She loved him.

When the thought entered her mind unbidden, she didn't start with surprise. She didn't question it. She knew its truth. She loved him. Not as a friend of many years, or as a child might worship an elder. She loved him for the man that he was: closed off, yes, still aloof and tightly composed. And while she did not understand him, she had witnessed glimpses of the humor, wit, and passion. Enough to ensnare her, body and soul.

"Well, then I suppose there is nothing for it but to marry the stubborn man," Kelly said aloud to herself. She chuckled at how practical and simple it sounded, when it was anything but practical or simple. Standing, she smoothed her dress and reached up, removing a handful of pins from her hair. She checked the effect in the mirror; hair partially pinned up, but with several thick, dark tendrils trailing over her back and shoulders. It was decidedly out of fashion, and she could already see her mother's scowling face in her mind's eye. But this was her battle, and she would be damned if she would wage it looking like someone other than herself.

Chapter 20

Theodore felt like a caged animal. Below him on the main floor of the townhouse, he could hear the muffled voices of an army of servants arranging final touches for the evening's ball. Through his open window, he could hear the gardener ordering around his assistants as they lit artfully placed candles. And inside his head, the voices of internal conflict were driving him mad. He didn't dare leave his apartments, so instead, he wore a path on the thick emerald-colored carpet as he paced restlessly back and forth.

Despite his attempts to put her off, his mother had played out her hand flawlessly. Without needing him to say a word yay or nay, she had led both Kelly's family and the ton at large to believe that he and Kelly would be married. Tonight was her pièce de résistance. He knew she hoped that after seeing Kelly in the role of wife, hostess, and presumptive countess, he would finally be swayed.

Damn her, that was not what this was about! What did he care if he had a woman to host balls and run his household? None of that was enough of a reason to subject both himself and Kelly to a marriage that would undoubtedly end in bitterness and disappointment. His mother was gracious and kind and loving, but his father had been cold and taciturn. He had seen the harsh consequences. What other outcome could possibly await him and Kelly? He had let this go too far already. Tonight, he decided, he would make it clear to his mother and to Kelly once and for all that this marriage was not going to happen.

He turned to the mirror on the wall and adjusted his cravat. His hand moved automatically to rake through his hair, but he stilled the impulse. *Control*, he reminded himself. He nodded resolutely and headed for the door. But before he could open it himself, there was an abrupt knock and it sprung open.

"My lord, you must come right away," His butler said urgently. He had never before entered Theo's chambers unbidden. A wave of cold swept through Theo. "It's Lady Eleanor."

Theo flew down the corridor. He heard the servant mumble something about sending out for the doctor but it didn't register. The door to his mother's room was open, and when he entered he saw her maid and the housekeeper at her bed, trying to get her to drink hot tea. Her breathing was coming in ragged, shallow bursts interrupted by fits of coughing.

He knelt by the side of the bed and took her hand in his. "Mother…" He was at a total loss for what to say. His mother had always been so steady. He knew she wasn't as well as she let on, but this seemed so much more serious than he had imagined. She was gasping for breath.

"Theo…I…" Eleanor tried to speak, but the effort erupted into another round of coughing. He squeezed her hand harder.

"Don't speak now, Mother. There will be time to talk after the doctor arrives." He took a couple of deep breaths and tried to make his voice sound confident and firm when she opened her mouth to speak again. "Do not argue. Not a word until the doctor says so. Focus on breathing." They sat there quietly hand in hand, both agonizing over each breath until the doctor arrived.

"Dr. Compton, I…" Theo began to speak, but the doctor held up his hand to forestall him.

"I'm familiar with your mother's condition, Lord Alston. I think it's best if you wait elsewhere while I examine her. I will be with you promptly." Dr. Compton, a wiry man in his late fifties, gave direction without hardly looking at Theo. He was already pushing his way to Eleanor's bedside and opening his medical bag.

"I will be in my private study, just down the hall." Theo managed to say. Dr. Compton nodded absently, his eyes not shifting from Eleanor.

Theo stared out the window, his hand gripped tightly around a glass of scotch that he had poured but hadn't drunk. In the time since he had left his mother's room, he had determinedly collected himself and regained control. He was logically considering immediate steps. The ball would have to be canceled; unfortunately, it was nearly time to begin, and he would be able to do nothing better than ask his staff to turn away guests at the door. Kelly would understand; he was sure she would want to stay and help, but he would send her home. He didn't want to expose her to the gossip that would surely ensure once news of the cancellation spread, nor ask her to do the duty of playing hostess. After all, she was not going to be his wife.

"Your mother is resting comfortably for now." Dr. Compton said immediately when he entered the room. Theo turned to the doctor but did not allow any reaction to play across his face.

"What is wrong with her?"

"She had an attack." Dr. Compton said slowly.

"What kind of attack? How long has this been going on? You said you were familiar with her condition, how is that so? Her doctor is Dr. Howell." He asked questions rapidly, his voice ringing with command.

But Dr. Compton was not easily intimidated. "I have been seeing Lady Eleanor since she arrived in London. Dr. Howell referred her to my care while she is staying in the city. As for the rest, I suggest you talk to your mother. It is her place to tell you, not mine." Theo immediately began to retort, but once again Dr. Compton stopped him. "She can talk to you now. Be mindful that you do not upset her. She must stay calm so that her breathing stays regular. I will call again tomorrow morning first thing to reassess her condition."

Theo nodded silently. As the doctor left, he finally brought his glass to his mouth and downed the amber liquid within. The burn in his throat helped him stay steady as he walked down the hall to his mother's bedroom.

Eleanor was reclining against her pillows. Her face was exceptionally pale, but her breathing was coming in soft, steady breaths. She held a steaming teacup in her lap, but her eyes were closed. Theodore entered silently, not wanting to disturb her. As he sat in the chair that the doctor had left at her bedside, her eyes flickered open.

"Theodore, don't look so cross." She said softly.

"I would not be cross if my own mother wasn't keeping secrets from me." He said, eyebrows raised. His mother's attempt at levity reassured him somewhat, but she was undeniably pale and weak.

"You didn't need to know," Eleanor answered matter-of-factly.

"I most certainly did. How long has this been going on?" Theo saw the stubborn set of her chin and knew she was contemplating not answering, but she must have thought better of it.

"It started about three years ago." She admitted.

"Three years! Mother, how could you have kept this a secret for so long? The doctor made it sound so serious!" Theodore felt his temper start to rise. His mother had always been fiercely on his side; together they had endured his father's cruel barbs and cold isolation. And yet she had been facing this alone? He was both angry that she had kept the secret, and hurt that she had not felt able to trust him with it. If their relationship wasn't sacred then nothing in his life made sense anymore.

"It is serious, Theodore. Now stop raging at me and listen." Eleanor's tone was rising to match her son's.

"Dr. Compton said you are not supposed to get upset, you need to calm down…" He started to say, but she interrupted him.

"Then be quiet and let me say my piece. I didn't tell you three years ago because I thought your marriage to Kelly was imminent. I didn't want to cast a cloud on you two. You always seemed so well-matched, and I wanted to afford you whatever happiness you might find together." As she talked, her voice leveled off. Ultimately, she was his mother, and she wanted more than anything to take away the pained look on his face. Theodore wanted to interrupt, but he didn't want to aggravate her symptoms, so he remained silent.

"However, you did not marry Miss Collins. And then another year passed, and still nothing, despite my repeated hints. So, when I heard Kelly and her mother had come to town, I went against Dr. Howell's wishes and followed. But enough is enough, Theodore. I want grandchildren while I still have a chance at being alive to see them." The desperation in her voice was evident.

It almost pained Theodore to respond: "Mother, you do not understand. It will not turn out well between Kelly and me."

"You and Kelly are not the same as your father and I."

"It isn't that simple. It is inevitable. I am too much like him."

Eleanor looked stricken. "You are *nothing* like your father, Theo,"

"I *am*, and he made sure of it." Theo saw the tears begin to well up in his mother's eyes, and he immediately regretted broaching this topic at all. He could see the pain in his mother's face. Damn it, he thought to himself. His father was gone, his ability to inflict suffering should have been as well.

"Please, Theo," She said sadly. "My lungs are damaged. They are not going to get better. Dr. Howell told me this years ago and Dr. Compton has confirmed it. If I am careful, I may have some years left. My dearest wish is to see you settled with Miss Collins, and to have the honor of meeting my grandchild." She saw Theodore visibly wince, but she didn't hesitate before finishing: "It is the only thing I have ever truly asked of you."

It was as if she had dealt a physical blow. Theo felt the air leave his body and his chest tighten. He owed his mother everything, it was as simple as that. If it had not been for her constant and unwavering love, he would have surely crumbled under his father's cold oppression.

Every logical, determined, disciplined part of Theo's mind screamed as he slowly nodded his head. "Alright, mother."

Chapter 21

*A*s Kelly and her mother mounted the stairs in front of the Alston townhouse, the door swung open readily. Kelly forced herself to smile through her nerves. "Good evening," She said warmly to Alston's butler as he closed the door behind them. But she knew immediately that something was wrong. His face was lined and ashen. "What has happened?"

"Lord Alston will explain." He said quietly as he guided them into the house. "Lady Collins, if you would wait in the parlor, Lord Alston would like to speak with Miss Collins in his private study." He motioned down the hallway to the parlor for Kelly's mother, and up the stairs for Kelly.

"That is not appropriate, sir. I must accompany my daughter." Claire Collins said, surprise and interest evident. Whatever new development there was, she wanted to hear about it firsthand.

"I am very sorry, my lady. But Lord Alston was very clear, he wishes to see Miss Collins alone for a few moments before their guests arrive. He said it is a critical matter for the success of the evening." The elderly man sounded like he was reciting a script. Kelly suspected that Theo had anticipated her mother's resistance and told him what to say.

"I'll be right along, Mother," Kelly said, starting for the stairs before her mother could protest further. "Bring my mother a cup of tea so she can relax before the chaos ensues. All will be well." She gave her mother a reassuring smile and silently willed her to go down the hall. Kelly had no idea what was going on, but she did know for certain that if her mother was with her, the likelihood of her getting an actual explanation from Theo was next to zero.

Claire reluctantly started down the hall to the parlor. Kelly nervously climbed to the second floor, wondering what was amiss. The house was buzzing with energy, but it didn't feel quite like the upbeat excitement of an imminent ball. She realized when she reached the top of the stairs that she didn't actually know where Theo's apartments were. The butler had stayed downstairs with her mother, and there were no other servants in sight. She peered in both directions and saw that a door was open down the hallway to her left.

She walked down the richly carpeted hall and peered inside. Theo was standing at the window, half turned away from her. Lord, he was handsome. His dark hair had gotten longer over the past few weeks, and curled ever so slightly around his collar. She couldn't see his piercing blue eyes in the dim light, but he was an impressive figure in his all-black ensemble and striking white cravat. On most men it would have looked austere; on him, it just enhanced his mystery and allure.

As he turned to look at her, she saw a series of emotions swim across his face. For a moment she thought she identified sadness, fear, yearning…and then his familiar mask of composure came down.

"Is everything alright, Theo? Your butler seemed quite put out…" Kelly trailed off uncertainly.

"My mother is not feeling well, she will not be able to join us tonight," Theo answered evenly, careful not to betray any emotion. He had spent the last few minutes trying to calm the tempest raging inside of him. The only way to manage so many feelings was to try and feel nothing at all.

"My goodness! I'm so sorry, Theo. If you need to be with her, mother and I can…"

"She will be fine. That is not what I want to speak to you about." Theo's voice was measured and careful. Kelly was beginning to know him well enough to detect that he was trying to keep a careful handle on his emotions, but she was not sure why. Theo moved closer to her and took her hand. He stared down at it for several long moments. The tension built between them until Kelly felt that if she struck a match, the pair of them would have burst into flame. Then Theo reached into his pocket and withdrew a sparkling ring. Without speaking, he slipped it onto her finger.

Kelly stared dumbfounded. The oval golden topaz stone was ringed by tiny diamonds. In the dim candlelight of the room, it seemed to glow. "This belonged to my mother. She wanted me to give it to you." Theo said quietly, still staring at her hand now adorned with the exquisite gem. Her gown was a bright copper color that enhanced her sparkling eyes and rich brown hair. Ironically his mother's ring seemed meant for Kelly on this night. It perfectly matched her ensemble. He seemed unable to speak, but when he turned his eyes up to meet hers, the question was in them.

"Yes," Kelly breathed without hesitation. In the next second, she found herself crushed against Theo, his lips taking hers hungrily and his arms holding her tightly against him.

Struggling to control the storm of emotions swirling through him, Theo poured himself into her kiss. He couldn't make sense of the pain and fear he felt for his mother, the mourning for his and Kelly's loss of freedom, or the strange lightness he had felt when she had accepted his silent proposal. This was not what he had wanted, for himself or Kelly. He was angry and resigned and confused. But his desire for Kelly was undeniable and he let it take control. He let himself bathe in the sweetness of her touch like a balm to his raw nerves.

Kelly reveled in the warmth and elation that spread throughout her body. She felt every curve of her body where it touched Theo's, the way the fabric created delightful friction as they moved against each other. She pressed her lips eagerly against him letting her tongue join his in a hot and searching dance. As her hands rubbed up and down his back and over his shoulders, she was delightfully aware of the warm circle of metal on her finger.

Finally, she thought to herself. She had sensed Theo's emotions when they had been together by the lake. Kelly knew that she loved him, but he was always so hard to read. It seemed that he was finally giving in to the emotions he had fought so hard against. He hadn't said that he loved her, but there was time for that. It would come. For now, it was enough that he had finally acknowledged that he did want her as his wife. Kelly felt no need to hold back anymore. She felt complete.

She ran her hands through his thick hair, pulling him closer to her and deepening their kiss. Instinctively, she arched her hips against his. Theo slid his hands down her back and cupped her bottom, pulling her tightly against him. Kelly responded by bringing her hands around to his cravat and beginning to loosen it. Inexperienced though she was, she knew that she desperately wanted to feel his skin against hers.

Slowly Theo began to realize where their encounter was leading. With all the strength and control he could muster, he slowly slid his hands back to Kelly's waist and eased her away from him. When he pulled his lips from hers, she looked up at him questioningly.

"Not now," He said. "We have to go downstairs. Guests will be arriving soon."

Kelly stared at him for another minute, her eyes searching his face, but she wasn't able to read it, and finally, she nodded. A smile spread across her face as she intertwined her hand with Theo's. "My mother will be waiting for us, we should tell her our good news."

Theo nodded, but he didn't return her smile. "We will make a formal announcement of our engagement at the ball tonight. We will marry one month hence." He said. His voice was even and flat. He didn't push

Kelly's hand away, but he didn't grip it back. Kelly felt something inside of her falter.

Without saying more, Theo led her from the study and down the hall to the stairway. She could hear the sound of carriages outside and the hum of voices. They had been away longer than she thought; guests were already beginning to spread throughout the lower level of the house. He started down the stairs, but Kelly paused and pulled back on his hand.

"Theo, is everything alright?" She asked him for the second time that evening. Theo didn't seem to be able to look directly at her. Moments ago, she had been suffused with happiness. But as she watched Theo, she felt seeds of doubt start to push their way to the surface.

Theo forced a smile onto his face. "Everything is fine, Kelly. You look beautiful. Let's go find your mother."

Chapter 22

*T*he sun streaming into her bedroom woke Kelly the next morning. She stretched luxuriously, and as she did the ring on her finger caught the sunlight and flashed across the ceiling. Slowly, she rotated her hand back and forth in the light, admiring how it shone. She wasn't usually one to have her head turned by jewelry or costly gifts. But this meant so much to her; it meant that Theo was going to be her husband. And his mother had given her blessing, giving him her own ring to propose to Kelly. *I must see her soon, to see how she is feeling and to thank her*, Kelly thought.

The ball had passed in a blur. She grinned as she recalled her mother's face when she had entered the room with Theo; how Claire's eyes had landed instantly on her hand and had widened and then shone with joy. Kelly had spent the night with her hand clasped in Theo's and her heart in her throat. She could hardly believe it had happened.

But it had. She stood next to Theo as he got the attention of the gathered crowd, and in a steady voice declared the engagement of himself, Lord Theodore Alston, Earl of Willingham, to Miss Kelly Collins of Middleborough. There had been a wave of hearty applause. Then she had stayed by Theo's side as they received congratulations from all their guests. Kelly and Theo had hardly exchanged words since they descended the stairs into the crush at the beginning of the evening, for they hadn't had a moment to themselves. There were a few times when Theo had seemed curt, especially when asked pressing questions. But that hadn't seemed to deter anyone; after all, Lord Alston was well known for his aloof manner. She suspected he was having a hard time adjusting to this new way of being, where feelings were given credence and value. It wasn't surprising to her that he was reverting to his more comfortable trope.

Kelly twirled a hand through her long hair as she spun the gold band around and around her finger, enjoying its warmth. Her misgivings from the night before had not gone away entirely, but she was actively choosing not to give way to them. She had seen him trying to hold his emotions at bay for weeks. She had felt the tenderness, warmth, and desire of his kiss. Of course, he would be awkward and unsure; giving reign to his feelings and agreeing to marry was a big decision for anyone, especially Theodore.

Kelly shivered delightfully at the memory of Theo's hands and lips upon her. "Alright, enough lazing about. There is a wedding to plan." She said to the sunlight, with one last indulgent stretch before pulling herself out of bed.

Theo was completely tied into knots. Dr. Compton had just left, reporting that Theo's mother Eleanor was recovering well, but cautioning that she should continue to rest and not become excited in any way. The ball had been an undeniable success; the *ton* had readily accepted his engagement. Kelly had sparkled, the picture-perfect lovestruck fiancée. He had felt numb the whole evening. And now, he felt a hundred things at once. Guilt, frustration, confusion.

"Good morning, my soon-to-be-married friend," Henry said with a jocular smile as he entered the room. He tossed his riding gloves onto one of the leather chairs and walked to pour himself a cup of tea from the tray in the corner. He completely missed Theo's dark look. "You should have seen Madison last night on the way home. I thought she was going to have a fit, she was so proud of herself. She takes personal credit for your successful engagement."

"Then she shouldn't be so quick to celebrate," Theo said dryly.

"What do you mean?" Henry frowned at the tone of Theo's voice and turned to look at his friend. He furrowed his eyebrows suspiciously, but as usual, he couldn't read Theo's face.

"It's a sham, Henry. It always was."

"Does this have something to do with that old chap I saw leaving when I arrived?" Henry asked, glancing meaningfully at the door through which Dr. Compton had left.

"Hmm," Theo skipped the tea and poured himself something stronger. "The doctor. My mother is ill. Her lungs are weak; she had an attack last night." He paused and took a steadying sip before continuing. "I only agreed to marry Kelly because my mother practically begged me to give her a grandchild before she dies."

Henry silently pursed his lips as he processed that information. "But Miss Collins certainly seemed elated, surely you must have given her some assurance of your feelings…"

"She doesn't know about mother," Theo answered, his voice tight.

"So…Miss Collins is under the impression that you changed your mind on your own, and that you genuinely want to marry her?"

"I suppose so."

"Oh god." Henry let out a deflated sigh.

"I know."

"Theo, you need to tell her." His friend said slowly.

"Absolutely not." Theo put his drink down with a solid thud. Henry resisted the urge to cringe outwardly.

"She will find out eventually, and then she will be devastated. You have nothing to lose by telling her now; she won't back out of the engagement. She was willing to marry you for the sake of the arrangement your fathers made. Why would she change her mind now?" Henry tried to reason.

"Damn it! This is the whole reason I didn't want to marry her in the first place! The first thing I do as her fiancé will be to hurt her? I won't do it. She has her reasons for marrying me, and I have my reasons for marrying her. Why does it need to be any more complicated than that?" Theo's frustration was evident. Henry had never seen it so visible, or Theo so vulnerable. Madison had been telling him for weeks that Theodore's heart was more involved in this than he was willing to admit. Henry was beginning to think that she was right.

"She cares for you, that is her reason. Bear that in mind, whatever you decide to do." Henry said grimly. *And you care for her*, he thought to himself, but he was wise enough not to add that thought out loud.

"Miss Collins, Lord Alston is here to see you," Augustine, the Collins' butler, opened the door to the parlor and admitted Theo without waiting for Kelly's approval. He had heard about the announcement, as had all of the Collins' household staff. They had known what was at stake, their own livelihoods as it were, and cheers had chorused through the lower levels of the house when the Collins ladies had returned the previous evening.

Theo saw Kelly's eyes light up when she saw him. She had foregone any kind of coiffure, and instead, her thick brown hair was long down her back, tied back simply off of her face with a ribbon. It should have made her look younger, but to Theo, it conjured images of what she might look like in the morning in her bed, with dark tendrils arrayed over her breasts.

Kelly smiled shyly, putting down the paper she had been attending to. "My mother has just gone out for the afternoon. She's going to confirm the date with the church and then have an announcement printed in the daily paper. She left me with the daunting task of working on the guestlist for the wedding breakfast," She said nodding to the writing desk where she had been sitting. Then she noticed something in his hand. "Are those for me?"

"Yes, of course," Theo held up the bouquet of flowers. He had bought them on a whim. He had never done something so impractical in his life. Maybe it was the guilt that he was feeling for not telling Kelly the truth when she had been so honest with him about her situation and feelings. Bringing flowers to one's fiancée was a completely sensible thing to do, he told himself. Guilt be damned.

"Thank you," Kelly took the flowers and smiled widely. Theo smiled back, but it wasn't the unabashed happiness that Kelly was feeling. His smile was slight, sultry, and sensual. "I hope, um…I hope you don't mind," She swallowed hard and tried to stop herself from mumbling. But suddenly she was nervous around Theo. His smile made her heart jump. "Mother going on with things. Lady Alston sent a note this morning telling her she ought to go ahead while she is unwell…"

Theodore nodded. "It's fine. The quicker we get everything taken care of, the better."

Kelly's breasts quivered as she let out a small chuckle and put her hand to her chest, an innocent action that stoked Theo like a fire. Instead of focusing on the untenable emotions swirling around them both, he was giving in fully to his physical desires.

"Yes, it's a lot to manage. I wanted to ask you, do you have any preferences…"

Theo couldn't resist her any longer. He put his arms around her and caught his hand in a stray tendril of hair resting on her shoulder. Kelly dropped the flowers in surprise. "Whatever you want." He whispered before taking her lips with his.

He moved his hands over her shoulders, back and bottom before tangling them in her hair and tugging back gently, exposing her neck to his kisses. She didn't realize she was moaning softly as he kissed behind her ear, down her neck to her collarbone, his tongue doing devilish and delicious things. When he started to move his lips back to hers, she boldly started to return the favor. She raked her hands through his hair as she had seen him do dozens of times over the years, feeling his thick, coarse locks between her fingers. The word *wanton* popped into her mind, but she didn't care. She loved Theo, and in a few short weeks, he would be her husband.

Theo groaned as she experimentally kissed along his jaw and the curve of his neck. She felt a little bit of stubble against her lips. How intimate it felt, to know this tiny detail of him so personally. "Kelly…" He said softly. He had completely lost control, but he didn't try and stop himself right away. It felt so damn good to get lost in her.

He felt himself hardening quickly and finally managed to pull himself away from her kisses. "God, Kelly," He exhaled forcefully.

"Did I do something wrong?" She asked worriedly, biting her lower lip.

"Quite the contrary," He said with a small laugh. "Creating an heir for the earldom with you isn't going to be a challenge at all." Kelly's faced clouded over, but Theo didn't notice. He was busy trying to calm his internal fires. "I should leave you to the planning before I do something rash." He bent over and retrieved the flowers she had dropped, handing them back to her. Kelly took them automatically. "I will see you soon."

Mistaking her quietness as her own attempt to control her raging desires, Theo gave her a quick kiss on the forehead and left. Kelly stared after him for a moment and then dropped down to the sofa. Her gaze shifted to the bouquet in her hand, but she barely processed the sight.

Creating an heir, he had said. Hadn't she used exactly that argument when trying to convince him of the sensibleness of them marrying? It hadn't been a compelling enough reason for him then. But something had changed his mind and now it was. Everything clicked into place; his sudden proposal, his aloof manner during the ball. He wasn't in love with her; the realization rolled through her like a storm front. He didn't really want to marry her at all.

She was devastated.

Chapter 23

*T*he carriage ride to the dressmaker's shop a week later was pure torture for Kelly. Her mother was babbling on happily, talking about the arrangements she had been making for the past several days. It had taken all of Kelly's energy to keep up a façade of excitement. The last week had been the longest of Kelly's life. The last thing she needed was for her mother to realize that something was amiss and add her worries to Kelly's already rampant ones.

But she didn't know how much longer she could keep the charade going. She had studiously avoided interacting with Theo in anything but the most formal, group settings. A family luncheon, tea with his mother and several of her friends, a ball. She had faked a headache when he called and asked to take her for a drive in the park. She was terrified that if she had a moment alone with him, she might break down entirely.

Her heart hurt. Not to mention her pride. She realized now that she had been foolish and naïve. Her feelings of love had blinded her and allowed her to convince herself of something that was not possible. What made her most frustrated was that she was getting exactly what she had said she wanted from the beginning. Theo would be her husband, and thereby she would ensure the wellbeing of her family, her estate, and all the people that depended on her.

But somewhere along the way, she had started wanting more. She didn't just want Theo as her husband, she wanted his love. She didn't just want him to desire her body, which he clearly did. She wanted him to desire her heart and mind as well. He was giving her exactly what she had asked him for all those weeks ago when she arrived in London, and yet now it didn't seem like enough.

But she had no other choice, as she had said to him again and again. Fulfillment of their marriage contract was the only answer to her problems. Well, the answer to her familial problems, anyway. It seemed that the problem of her heart was just one she was going to have to live with.

The carriage lurched to a stop and Kelly followed her mother inside. They were immediately greeted by a young shopgirl dressed in black, her hair pinned back neatly under a white cap. "Lady Collins, Miss Collins," she bobbed a curtsey. "If you'll come right this way, Madame Janine will be with you momentarily. Lady Warsham has already arrived." They were led to a private parlor, where Madison was already seated and sipping tea. When she saw them, she jumped to her feet excitedly, nearly upsetting the table and steaming pot.

"Lady Collins," Madison touched cheeks familiarly with Kelly's mother Claire, making her blush. Their growing acquaintance with Madison and her husband had conferred considerable status on their family, and Lady Collins was still not used to Madison's warm manner. "Oh Kelly, I am bursting with excitement!" Madison said as she turned to Kelly and grabbed her hands. She pulled her enthusiastically down to the settee, where there was already an array of swatches of fabric laid out.

"Madame Janine doesn't usually take commissions on this short of a timeline, but I insisted. I have spent enough of Henry's money in her shop over the past few years that she could hardly deny me." Madison winked broadly at Claire and Kelly.

As Madison started pouring tea for them, a very tall older woman swept into the room. She was dressed in black as the shop girl had been, but the fabric was rich and the dress exquisite. She exuded authority and confidence. "Lady Warsham," She greeted Madison first, her longtime client and the highest-ranked person in the room.

"Ah, Madame Janine!" Madison smiled brightly. "May I present my dear friend, Miss Kelly Collins, and her mother, Lady Collins, Baroness Middleborough." She grabbed Kelly's hand and dragged her forward. "Our lovely bride needs a new gown for her wedding…less than three weeks hence."

"Lady Collins, Miss Collins," Madame Janine curtsied slightly. She looked less than convinced. "Yes, your correspondence did mention the particulars of your request. This is very short notice, Lady Warsham. I don't know what can be done in such a short time."

"I really can wear something I already have; the gowns from my come-out have hardly seen the light of day in the last few years," Kelly interjected, but Madison was already shaking her head.

"No, no, Kelly, that won't do. You are going to be the Countess of Willingham. I'm hardly a stickler for propriety, you know that, but this is your wedding. You should at least have a new gown."

Kelly's mother was nodding along. "I do agree with Lady Warsham. Appearances are important." Kelly resisted the urge to roll her eyes.

Madame Janine made a show of being flustered, but eventually, Madison cajoled her into an agreement. "There isn't time to order anything; we will have to make do with items I already have on hand." She made a motion of her hand and two assistants appeared as if out of thin air. They had clearly been on hand, Madame Janine's resistance token. "Girls, fetch our selection of lace, and samples of anything that would be appropriate for the wedding of a *countess*, silk taffeta will do nicely I think."

Her stomach still in knots, Kelly accepted a cup of tea from Madison and sat on the sofa. She observed the parade of fabrics and accouterments without enthusiasm. Luckily, Madison and her mother had strong opinions and dismissed many things right off.

"I don't think yellow would be the most complementary color to her skin, don't you think, Lady Collins?" Madison waved away several proffered silks, and Claire Collins nodded her agreement.

"This lace is very lovely; it would look nice around the hem and perhaps a touch on the sleeves?" Claire said, glancing up at Madame Janine for input. The designer nodded approvingly. Kelly's mother looked to her. "What do you think, Kelly?

"I…um…I…" Kelly stumbled over her words, looking down at her hands and sighing deeply.

"Whatever is wrong, Kelly? You've been out of sorts all morning," Her mother looked at her worriedly, and Kelly did her best to straighten herself up.

"I'm…I'm perfectly well," She managed to get out. "I did not sleep well last night, that is all. I like the lace." She added, though she knew her voice was hollow.

Madison's brow furrowed. "Kelly, let's have a closer look at those over there, maybe we were too hasty to discard them." Indicating a stack of fabric set down on a table on the other side of the parlor, Madison drew Kelly along with her away from Lady Collins and Madame Janine. The two older women stayed behind and continued to debate the perfect lace from the selections available.

"I do like the pink one, I suppose," Kelly said, fingering one of the bolts of silky fabric.

"Let that be for now," Madison said dismissively. "Out with it, what's troubling you?" She asked quietly.

"Nothing…really…I am just overtired from all the planning and preparations," Kelly said, not able to meet Madison's eyes.

"Kelly…" Madison took her friend's hand. "There is more to it, isn't there? On the night you and Theo announced your engagement you were practically glowing. But every time I've seen you since, it's like the light has gone out. If you have been sleeping that poorly every single night, perhaps you need to see a physician about a sleep tonic." She attempted to tease, but the concern in her voice was obvious.

"Madison, I…" Kelly wanted to share her burden, but she didn't even know where to start. She had made such a mess of things.

"It's something to do with Theo, yes? I warned him not to toy with your emotions," Madison started.

"It's not as if he hasn't been perfectly honest with me from the start," Kelly said bitterly. "I should have known better than to let my feelings for him grow, but I just couldn't stop myself. I…well, I…" Her voice broke.

"You love him," Madison said gently.

"Yes," Kelly whispered sadly. "And I thought he loved me. But I was a fool, he doesn't want to marry me. All he wants is an heir." The words tumbled out of Kelly, and as they did she felt a wave of relief flow through her. Just speaking the words aloud, telling them to someone else, was more soothing than she could have anticipated.

Now it was Madison's turn to sigh deeply. Kelly saw that she looked conflicted, but eventually, she made up her mind to speak. "Love and marriage… are complicated for Theodore. Henry hasn't told me everything, he would never break Theo's confidence of course. But, I wouldn't lose hope just yet."

Kelly's eyebrows shot up. "What do you mean?" She asked cautiously. "What do you know that I do not? What has he said?"

Madison shook her head. "I am not sure of everything, and I do not want to mislead you with my speculation. I have come to know Theodore well these past several years, and I think I can connect the dots.

But you should hear it from the horse's mouth, as they say."

"Theo will never open up to me. I have been trying for weeks, months, years it seems like. He has decided to close himself off." Kelly said defeatedly.

"Perhaps you should talk to his mother," Madison suggested.

"Lady Alston? What does she have to do with any of this?"

Giving a small shrug, Madison squeezed Kelly's hand. "I really think you should ask her. There is perhaps nobody in the world who knows Theo better."

Kelly nodded. Madison was right about that; while Theo was so often closed off to her, she had observed the genuine love and regard between mother and son on many occasions. Perhaps his mother would be willing to share with her, if only out of a desire to see Theo happy himself.

Madison smiled encouragingly and then turned back to the table before them. "Now, you said you liked the pink, and I think you are completely correct. This color looks lovely against your skin." Without missing a beat, Madison held up the pale pink silk. Kelly felt a small smile turn up the corners of her lips, and a flicker of hope light inside of her.

Chapter 24

$\mathcal{I}$t took Kelly several more days to work up the nerve to go and talk to Lady Alston. Getting away from her mother long enough and with a reasonable excuse was difficult in itself. Finally, an opportunity presented itself, and Kelly forced herself to seize upon it.

"I need Lady Alston's finalized guest list for the wedding breakfast so that invitations can go out tomorrow, but I am scheduled to meet with the florist to finalize the arrangements for the church in half an hour." Claire frowned and put her hands on her hips, clearly bemused at how she could have gotten herself into such a conundrum. "I suppose I could send over a groom with the message to Lady Alston, though I don't want her to think it a sign of disrespect…" she trailed off, her frown deepening.

Kelly saw her chance. "I can call upon Lady Alston," She said quickly.

Her mother paused; Kelly had been less than enthusiastically engaged in the planning process. But there wasn't any reason not to send Kelly, and it would allay her current problem. "Yes, alright." She nodded. "Do try and remind her that our house is not as grand as hers; we cannot accommodate too many guests. But be respectful! We do not want to offend her; we can always cut some of our guests if it is absolutely essential."

Kelly doubted Lady Alston would be offended. In all of their recent interactions, she had come across as eminently reasonable. But she humored her mother and nodded somberly. "I will be most reverential, the model of a dutiful daughter-in-law." She said. Her mother narrowed her eyes, suspecting she was being mocked, but decided to let it go.

"Off you go, then. As I said, those invitations need to go out tomorrow at the absolute latest."

Thoroughly dismissed, Kelly gathered herself, summoned a carriage, and got on her way to the Alston home. She was quickly admitted and shown to the morning room.

She sat nervously with her hands folded in her lap. Today could be a turning point; perhaps she would finally start to unlock the doors that separated her and Theo. Maybe, just maybe, there was hope for them yet.

"Yes, have my horse saddled. I'm going to fetch one item from in here and then I shall be along," Theo called over his shoulder as he strode into the room. He was startled when he turned his head and saw Kelly perched on the edge of one of the chairs. "Kelly…I…Miss Collins…"

"Usually I'm the one stammering," Kelly quipped.

Theo chuckled. "Indeed. I admit you have caught me unawares this morning. I didn't know you were here." He lowered himself to the chair next to her. Lord, it was good to see her. Especially alone. It seemed the only times he had seen her in the past weeks had been at one public social function or another. He was by no means happy about their impending wedding, but he no longer saw the point in trying to suppress the attraction he felt for Kelly. "I can delay my outing and stay awhile if you like…" His smile was heavy with implication.

"I am not here to see you," Kelly said frostily. Theo drew back immediately. "I'm here to see Lady Alston about preparations for the wedding breakfast." Her tone was even and flat. Carefully controlled. Where was this coming from, Theo thought? The last time they had spoken, alone at least, had been the day he had brought her flowers. She had been sweet and open then, and perfectly polite in their public meetings since. What had brought about this change?

Although she was waiting on tenterhooks to speak to Theo's mother, Kelly was unwilling to give reign to the spark of hope that Madison had lit inside of her. All she wanted at this moment was to melt into Theo's arms, allow him to kiss her, and soothe her. But she didn't dare let herself be that vulnerable. Her heart, her entire happiness, was hanging in the balance.

"I hope I haven't done anything to upset you, Kelly?" Theo said carefully, watching her face for any clue. Kelly was usually an open book when it came to her emotions. But her face betrayed nothing. *Bravo*, he thought sarcastically. She had learned well from him.

"Not at all, Lord Alston." Kelly felt her voice quivering. Keeping up the careful façade took a painstaking effort. She felt a small twinge of pity for Theo, who had spent years wearing this armor.

Theo waited for her to say something more, but she avoided his gaze and looked down at her hands. "Well, then I shall see you later." He stood up, pausing for one more awkward moment. "Good day, Miss Collins." Then he walked out of the room, forcing himself not to glance back over his shoulder.

Kelly fought back tears. She had never felt such conflicting emotions: love and longing for Theo, despair over the distance between them, fear that she might never fulfill the future she dreamed of for them.

Theo's mother entered the room quietly. Kelly did not notice her immediately, which gave the older woman an unguarded view of the younger's emotions. She did not know Kelly very well yet, but the heavy feelings were evident in her hunched shoulders, her trembling hands, and her flushed cheeks. Eleanor felt sorry for her; she knew that Theo was not an easy man to love. He made it difficult in almost every way. And she suspected that love was exactly what young Kelly was suffering from.

"Ah, Kelly, good morning." She said as she slowly made her way across the room. Kelly straightened up immediately and forced a smile onto her face.

"Good morning, Lady Alston. I hope you are feeling well today?" Kelly asked, genuine concern showing in her face.

"I am well enough. I have to slow down a bit, which is decidedly out of character." The older woman smiled kindly, settling herself onto the sofa adjacent to Kelly. "You needn't go on calling me Lady Alston. Eleanor is fine, or perhaps even Mother Eleanor if you like."

"Of course, Mother Eleanor." Kelly smiled despite her nervousness. No matter what happened with her

and Theo, it seemed she would have a friend in the
dowager countess.

"I like the sound of that," Eleanor said. "Now, I
suppose your mother has sent you about the guestlist
for the wedding breakfast? Is she quite worked up?"

"Oh, no, of course not," Kelly said quickly, a little
embarrassed. "She is just…um…"

Eleanor smiled knowingly. "You are her only
daughter, Kelly. And your mother always has been
the anxious sort. Do not worry, my dear, she is
entitled to her excitement."

Kelly nodded, trying to muster up the gumption to
address her real purpose. "Lady Alston…Mother
Eleanor…" She mumbled. "My mother did send me
about the wedding, but there is something else I
would like to ask you about."

Eleanor's eyebrows raised speculatively. "Oh?
What is it, dear?"

"Well…Madison said that perhaps…you know
how aloof Theo is…and he has been so contrary to
our marriage…" Kelly struggled to get the words out.
Honestly, she wasn't even sure exactly what to ask.

Eleanor sighed deeply. "I think I understand your
meaning. If you will forgive me, I saw you when I first
came in and you seemed…upset. Perhaps you can
give me a little insight?"

"Well, Theo has just…it has been so difficult…I
don't want you to think that I think ill of Theo…"
Kelly continued to stammer, but Eleanor reached
over and took her hands in her own.

"Kelly, I think it would be best if we didn't try to
dance around things. It is plain to me that you adore
Theodore. You always have." She squeezed Kelly's

hand tightly. Kelly felt the tension start to flow out of her.

"I love him." She said plainly. "I love him so much."

Eleanor's satisfaction was clear. "I suspected as much."

"But he does not love me. Or maybe he won't let himself love me." Kelly began. "You see, when he proposed to me at the ball, I really thought he had changed his mind. I had seen flashes of it before. He was trying to keep his emotions under control, but it sometimes seemed that he was developing a true affection for me. So, when he gave me your ring, I thought he had finally realized that he loved me as well."

"Did he say something to that effect?" Eleanor asked interestedly.

"No," Kelly admitted. "But I just thought he wasn't ready yet. That he wanted to marry me, but couldn't bring himself to say it yet. I was alright with that, I was willing to let him say it in his own time. But later…he said something else, and I realized I was wrong. He doesn't want to marry me. Not at all." She finished bitterly.

Eleanor was silent for what seemed like an eternity, and Kelly wondered if she had shared too much. When she finally spoke, her voice was laced with sadness. "I think I should tell you about my marriage to Theo's father."

Kelly looked up questioningly. Whatever did that have to do with this?

Taking a fortifying breath, Eleanor continued. Though Kelly did not think of her as old, as she began to speak it seemed like her face aged instantly. "I was quite young when we married, only seventeen years old. Theodore's father ten years older. He wasn't eager for marriage, but he knew it was his duty to marry and continue the lineage. So when his father arranged the union, he didn't protest. At first, I was smitten. He was quite handsome, if you remember, much like Theo.

"But things changed quickly. Beyond creating an heir, the elder Lord Alston did not have much use for me. My own parents' union had been cordial, not a love match but there was genuine affection. I expected as much for myself. But Theo's father was cold, distant. I thought if I pushed hard enough, I could break through that layer of him and find the warmth beneath."

"He sounds a lot like Theodore," Kelly said softly, bemused.

"No," Theo's mother said sharply. "Theodore certainly thinks so, but it is not true. I tried and tried to build something with his father, but there was nothing there to find. He was cold to the core, and when I tried to find something else within him, he mocked me cruelly. From then on there was nothing but ice and harsh words between us.

"Theo may seem hard and cold, but there is so much more to him than that. He had to build up that wall to protect himself from his father. But from the moment Theo was born, he knew my love and he returned it without restraint. That is something his father never had the capacity to do."

"I thought that when he went away to boarding school, that was what changed him. We had always been so close, and then suddenly it was like he was a different person altogether." Kelly said.

"I sent him to school at Harrow so that he would not have to spend every waking moment under his father's tyranny. I wanted to protect him, and he learned quickly to keep his guard up when he was home so his father could not make his life more difficult." Eleanor explained. "I regret that it created a rift between you." She said earnestly.

Kelly shook her head. "You did what you had to do; I see that now in a way I never did before."

"Thank you," Eleanor nodded. "And now I have to admit what I am not proud of, for it was a manipulation on my part. I hope you will forgive an old woman's meddling; I thought it for the best."

Kelly swallowed apprehensively, but inclined her head slightly to indicate that Eleanor should continue.

"On the evening of the ball, I had an attack. I have been unwell for some time and sometimes suffer from attacks where I cannot breathe properly. Theodore did not know this, and he was quite shaken by the incident. In that moment, I took advantage of his feelings. In his moment of vulnerability, I asked him to honor your betrothal, and give me the grandchildren I so desperately desire."

Kelly drew back in surprise. "That is why he changed his mind," the realization hitting her like a punch in the gut. "I knew he did not love me…but…" But it was another thing to hear it so matter-of-factly.

"I don't believe that for a moment," Eleanor said fiercely, grabbing back Kelly's hands. "Please believe me when I say this, Kelly: Theodore feels everything very deeply. He always has. He keeps his mask in place to protect himself. He sees marriage as an inevitable state of misery. He truly believes that any marriage will devolve into something like his father and me."

"But he only agreed to marry me because…" Kelly started but Eleanor interjected.

"He fought so hard against marrying you because he cares about you profoundly. If he did not, it wouldn't matter because he wouldn't fear hurting you. But I believe he cannot bear the thought of causing you the kind of pain that his father caused for me, and so he will not let himself get close to you."

"But Theo would never hurt me, not intentionally, I know that," Kelly protested.

"You know that, and I know that, but Theodore does not know it. He does not believe it." Eleanor said. She patted the unoccupied bit of the sofa next to her, imploring Kelly to come sit closer. Kelly did as she bid, sitting knee to knee with the mother of the man she loved so desperately.

"And now I must ask you to do something which seems impossibly difficult," Eleanor said solemnly. "Do not give up on him Kelly, I beg you. I can see the pain that it is causing you, to love him and not have that love returned openly. But if you truly love him…"

"I do." Kelly interrupted without hesitation. "I do love him. And I will not give up. I had no idea what you might say when I came here today. I certainly didn't expect to learn so much," she admitted. Kelly's eyes brimmed with tears, and Eleanor's did as well. "I was afraid to hope before. But you have made me see that perhaps there is something to hope for after all."

Chapter 25

The week of their wedding came upon them quicker than either Kelly or Theo expected. Suddenly, all of the details had been settled and all that was left to do was wait for the appointed day. As Kelly attended her final dress fitting with Madison at Madame Janine's shop, Theodore was engaged in a round of billiards in his gentleman's club with Henry.

"Of course I'll stand up with you as your best man," Henry chuckled and clapped Theo on the shoulder. "Leaving the asking a bit late though, aren't you?"

Theo shrugged, pointing his cue to take another shot. "Honestly I hadn't thought of it until my mother asked me. She and Kelly's mother have taken care of all of the details. It is as if the wedding has taken on a life of its own without any help from me." As if mirroring his mood, the ball bounced off of the side of the table and missed the pocket entirely.

"That is how weddings go," Henry commiserated. "Dare I ask how things are between yourself and Miss Collins?" He took a shot that went directly in.

"I'd rather you didn't."

"Well, unfortunately for you…"

"Things are fine," Theo said shortly, but then he sighed in resignation. "I don't know what is going through her head. She seemed thrilled initially, but then the last time I saw her she was very brief with me."

"Perhaps she suspects that you are not wholly committed to your union?" Henry suggested.

"There is no way she would know about that." Theodore shook his head and lined up his next shot. "I suppose it is just nerves. It is one thing to talk about marriage, and another to be facing the thing head-on. I know that well enough myself." The ball missed again, and Theodore looked miserable.

Unsure of what else to say, Henry put his cue up on the rack and motioned to the door. "Come have supper with us. Madison is always good for a laugh."

"I'm sure that I am not the best company right now. Plus, I am about to beat you." He said drolly, eyeing the many balls still on the table.

"Unlikely," Henry mocked lightly. "Madison is used to your dour moods. Let's go."

Begrudgingly, Theodore put down his cue and followed Henry out the door.

"It is just lovely," Madison said simply as Kelly walked out from behind the curtain to reveal herself in the gown that Madame Janine had created especially for her. The pale pink color made her cheeks look rosy and bright, and complemented her brown hair and eyes beautifully. Kelly couldn't help twirling a bit side to side as she looked at her reflection in the full-length mirror, admiring the way the fabric shimmered ever so slightly.

"It really is," Kelly agreed. "Please give Madame Janine my many, many thanks." She said to the young assistant who was leaning down to pin the hemline.

"Of course, miss. If you give me just a moment, I will pin this so we can perfect the length. Everything else looks just right." The young woman said, getting right to her task.

"You seem much more...peaceful," Madison said probingly. "How did your talk with Lady Alston go?"

"It was very...enlightening," Kelly said, struggling for a moment to think of the right word. She felt honored that Eleanor had opened up to her so completely about herself and Theo's past, and she wanted to be careful to respect their privacy.

"Did you get the answers you needed?"

"I feel that I understand Theodore better, and that was what was most important," Kelly said, stepping down from the pedestal and behind the curtain so the assistant could help her remove the delicate garment.

Coming out again once fully dressed, she added "I don't know what the future holds for Theo and me. But I love him, and God willing, I will do everything in my power to build a happy marriage between us."

Madison smiled. She wanted nothing more for Kelly and Theo, who had both become very dear to her heart in their own rights. "How about you come home to supper with me? We can send a note along to your mother so she doesn't worry. We can celebrate with some of the good sherry that I have stashed away." Madison winked playfully.

Kelly couldn't help laughing. "Alright then, that does sound nice." Putting her arm through her friend's, they headed out of the shop to the waiting carriage outside.

"Is Henry at home?" Madison asked her butler as she handed her pelisse to a neatly attired maid.

"Yes, my lady. Lord Warsham and Lord Alston are in the study at the moment." He replied promptly. Madison's eyebrows raised in surprise and she turned to face Kelly.

"Well, this is an unexpected development," She said with a grin.

Kelly's eyes narrowed. "You planned this, didn't you?"

Madison laughed. "Usually this is exactly my kind of maneuver, but this time it is completely coincidental." She said honestly. She saw Kelly holding back apprehensively, and smiled encouragingly. "Best start as we mean to carry on, don't you think?"

"I suppose you are right," Kelly agreed, following Madison slowly down the hallway.

Madison pushed open the door without a knock or the slightest hesitation. "Good evening gentlemen!" She said brightly. "Henry, darling, it seems like we both had the same idea to invite guests for supper tonight."

Henry laughed, as both Kelly and Theo tensed at the sight of one another. "So it would seem," he said. "Theo and I were just having a pre-supper libation. Should I ring for tea for you ladies?"

Madison scoffed. "Hardly, call for the good sherry. Kelly and I are celebrating that the wedding preparations are completed at last."

Henry smiled indulgently and did as his wife asked. "So, Kelly, are you feeling relieved that everything is taken care of?" He asked conversationally.

"Um, yes," She answered. "Truthfully, my mother has done most of the planning. I've just had to bob my head 'yes' or 'no.'"

"At least your mother has asked your opinion," Madison said. "My mother had a vision in her head of her daughter's dream wedding and would not allow me to contradict her in the slightest." She rolled her eyes. "Theo, has your mother been quite opinionated?" She said, obviously trying to draw Theo into the conversation.

Theo shrugged noncommittally. "It seems like she and Lady Collins have gotten on easily enough."

The conversation threatened to die there, as both Henry and Madison waited for Kelly or Theo to pick it up. After a few leaden moments, Madison broke the silence.

"Henry, do come with me for a moment. I need your opinion as we confer with the steward about the wine selection for tonight's meal, now that we have guests." Henry followed her out of the room, leaving Theodore and Kelly in awkward quiet.

Kelly picked up the glass of sherry that had been poured for her and sipped at it. Theo had taken up a position leaning against the mantle of the large fireplace a few paces away. He was staring at her, trying to think what his next move should be. Finally, he said: "I want to apologize for whatever it is that I said or did to upset you last time we were together."

"Oh no! Please don't think anything of it." Kelly said quickly. She managed to smile at him through her nerves. "I wasn't feeling quite myself. But I am feeling much better now."

Encouraged, Theo returned her smile. He was drawn to her like a magnet, crossing the few steps between them and sitting down next to her. "I was thinking that after the wedding breakfast, we could go back to Willingham Park for a week or two. Have a sort of impromptu honeymoon, as it were."

"I don't know if it counts as a honeymoon if we are among servants and rooms we have both known our whole lives." Kelly teased.

"I can try to arrange something more adventurous if you would like, but it is short notice at this point." He offered, enjoying how easy it seemed between them.

"No," Kelly shook her head, her lips forming a little pink circle. Theo could feel the warmth of her body and became startlingly aware of the up and down of her breasts as she breathed. "I want to start creating happy memories at Willingham Park as soon as possible." *To start erasing the painful ones,* she finished in her mind.

Theo leaned over to kiss her, and Kelly's eyes flitted closed expectantly. However, they were interrupted when the door to the study swung open loudly. They sprang apart automatically as if caught. Henry and Madison came quickly through the doorway.

"A messenger just arrived from my sister, Leonora. Her husband was in some sort of riding accident." The dismay on her face was clear; though this might any other time be 'her kind of maneuver' as she had said earlier, her honesty in the moment was undeniable. "I am so sorry, but we have to leave right away."

Kelly and Theodore stood up immediately. Kelly embraced her friend. "We will go now, do not worry about us. I am sure that Theodore can see me home." Theo was already nodding acquiesce.

"No, please." Henry intervened. "Supper is already being laid out, it would be a waste if no one were to enjoy it. Besides, I'm sure everything will be fine, and we may even be back to join you before supper is over." He put his arm around his wife reassuringly and began to guide her out of the room. "We will see you both soon." He said over his shoulder.

Chapter 26

*J*ust like that, Theodore and Kelly were alone. They stared after their friends, unsure of what to do or say next. The Warsham's butler appeared in the doorway, saving them from their indecision. "Supper is ready, Lord Alston, Miss Collins," He nodded politely at each of them and motioned out the door to the dining room.

"Shall we?" Theo said, standing and offering Kelly his arm.

"I suppose so," She said, putting her hand warmly on his and letting him escort her out.

Supper started awkwardly. Theo didn't want to disrupt the tentative truce that had been called between them, while also trying to manage his urges to lean across the table and take Kelly into his lap. For her part, Kelly was seeing Theo in an entirely different light. Before she had seen his stoic distance as a personal affront, but not she saw it for what it was: his attempt to protect himself from any pain. It made his kind overtures to her all the sweeter. Despite his staunch efforts to keep up walls between them, his resolve was weakening. She also was not immune to the heady look in Theo's eyes. His desire for her was almost tangible, and she felt all of the most private parts of her body heat in response.

As the courses progressed, the awkwardness dissolved. Kelly felt herself relaxing and truly enjoying Theo's company. When the household staff cleared away dessert, Kelly realized that it was time for her leave. Madison and Henry were clearly not returning, and the private meal she and Theo had enjoyed was highly improper in itself. To linger any longer would be nothing short of scandalous.

"Will you join me for a glass of that sherry?" The suggestion in Theo's voice was clear. He was staring directly into Kelly's eyes, and the tension between them was fierce.

"Perhaps just some tea," Kelly said, the words coming out of her mouth before she could stop them. She knew better; knew that this was entirely improper. But she followed Theo back into the study without hesitation.

The instant the door closed behind them, they were in each other's arms. Theo's tongue slid sensually against Kelly's lips, and she opened her mouth to meet him readily. His kiss was so tender, Kelly could practically feel the longing for love and closeness that Theo emanated. His mind might not know what it wanted or needed, but his body certainly did. And Kelly was ready to give openly to the man she loved.

When he started to unlace her gown, she didn't protest. She turned around so that he could more easily access the laces. Theo seized on the opportunity, running his lips down her neck and shoulder as his hands worked. Kelly shivered delightfully as her gown slid to a puddle on the floor, and Theo's hands ran up and down the front of her body, caressing her hips and breasts. She could feel his hardness pressing against her from behind.

She turned around and ran her hands along his chest under his coat. Then she pushed the coat up over his shoulders and away. She struggled with his cravat, and he smoothly helped her divest him of the silk tie and shirt.

Theo lowered her to the leather sofa, kissing her breasts as he pulled at the ribbons of her chemise to reveal her soft, full mounds. Slowly he licked and drew each nipple into his mouth, sucking until Kelly was moaning and arching against him. Hearing her moan, Theo could resist no longer.

"Oh Kelly," he moaned. In one last moment of coherency, he managed to ask: "Are you sure?"

She didn't pause a moment. "Yes," Kelly breathed heavily.

He reached down and freed himself of his breeches. Slowly he slid inside of her, mindful of her virginity. But she pressed against him eagerly and he struggled to restrain himself. She cried out suddenly, a little yelp of pain. And then she was moving with him again, caught up in the pleasurable sensations of his hard length inside her tightness.

Kelly had never felt something so completely right. It was as if she and Theo were one; it was what she had longed for. She felt the intensity building. There couldn't possibly be more than this? And then waves of gratification were washing over her. She heard herself moaning, and then Theo joined her, his satisfaction matching her own. His hips slowed, and he let out a long, deep sigh.

For long minutes Kelly lay there in Theo's arms. He softly kissed her hair, neck, and shoulder. She reveled in the warmth of his body, the entire length of it still pressed against hers. "Theo…" she whispered lovingly.

"Hmm?" He ran his hand over her stomach, making her shiver anew. "I suppose we absolutely must be wed now." He said lightly. Where Kelly might have once taken offense, she now saw him trying to make light of the situation to mask his emotions.

She rolled over to face him. The sofa where they lay was not large, so the action brought their bodies even closer together. She reached up tenderly and ran her hand along his cheek and jaw. "It's alright now, Theo. We have each other. You don't have to guard yourself with me," she said softly.

Theo drew back so her could better see her face. "What do you mean by that?" He asked, his brow furrowing.

"Only that you can trust me," She answered. "Theo…I know things have been difficult for you, and you haven't always seen the best parts of a relationship, but…"

"What are you talking about?" Theo sat up now, putting more distance between them unconsciously.

"I…" Kelly hesitated, but couldn't help but be honest. "Your mother told me about how it was with your father, and…"

"You spoke to my mother about me?" His face reddened, with embarrassment or anger Kelly wasn't sure, but the betrayal in his voice was unmistakable.

The warmth and closeness that had been between them moments before were evaporating at an alarming rate.

"I only wanted to better understand, Theo," Kelly said defensively.

"You had no right to interfere like that!" Theo stood up, yanking on his breeches and reaching for his shirt.

"Theo, I was trying to help…" She trailed off pitifully as he pulled his shirt over his head and threw his waistcoat over his arm.

"This was a mistake," Theo said angrily. And without another word, he stormed out of the room, the door closing with a sharp thud behind him.

Kelly stared at the door in complete shock. Looking around her, she took in her naked skin and her clothing strewn on the floor. She could hardly process what had just happened. One moment she had felt closer to Theo than ever before, and then suddenly…she had never felt so alone. Fighting back tears, she hastily dressed and fled with what was left of her pride.

Chapter 27

wo days later, Theodore stood woodenly with his mother in the entry hall of their townhouse, waiting to welcome Kelly and her family. Kelly's father, Baron of Middleborough, had arrived in London the day before. Their mothers had arranged this informal dinner on the eve of the wedding so that everyone could become reacquainted. Madison and Henry would also be in attendance, as they would be standing up as the best man and matron-of-honor the next day.

The Warshams arrived first and were greeted warmly by Lady Alston. "I was so sorry to hear about your sister's husband, Lady Warsham. Theo told me there was an accident." Eleanor said kindly.

Madison gave a small smile of thanks. "He will make a full recovery, it seems, but he certainly gave Leonora a fright." She turned her gaze to Theo. She hadn't had a chance to speak to Kelly since she and Henry had hurried away a few evenings before, and her servants were attempting to be discrete. But she sensed that some sort of incident had occurred. "All's well, Theodore?" She said archly.

"Of course," He answered without emotion and avoided her gaze. Madison narrowed her eyes but didn't push further. She heard the Collins' arriving behind them.

"Lady Alston, I am so pleased to see you again. It has been so long; much too long!" Kelly's father said as he entered, grasping Eleanor's hand and smiling. Lady Alston returned his smile warmly.

"It is so nice to finally have things coming to rights after all these years, is it not?" Theo's mother said, satisfaction evident in her voice.

"Indeed, it is," Kelly's mother, Claire, chimed in, greeting Lady Alston and then offering her hand to Theo, who took it and greeted her automatically.

"Ah, Kelly, you look lovely," Eleanor turned her eyes on the bride-to-be. "Doesn't she look beautiful, Theodore? The perfect image of a blushing bride."

Kelly did blush, but not for the reasons her mother-in-law-to-be imagined. She was so embarrassed; she had given herself so completely to Theo and he had rebuffed her. She had no idea what to do now, but she knew that she wished she was anywhere but there.

Luckily, their parents were so pleased with themselves they didn't seem to notice Kelly and Theo's discomfort. The party proceeded into the parlor, and Kelly followed closely behind her mother to avoid being alone with Theo. She could have sworn she heard him mutter the word "*coward*" as he followed her into the room. But she gritted her teeth and ignored him.

"Will you being going back to Middleborough immediately, Lord Collins, or will you be staying in

London for a while?" Henry asked Kelly's father as they were seated for dinner.

"I think I will stay a few days in the Capitol. It has been years since I've spent any time here." He answered. "Besides, I heard that Lord Alston plans on taking Kelly to Willingham Park following the wedding breakfast tomorrow, and I thought it would be nice to give them some privacy. The estates are right next to each other."

"That sounds nice; I've never been to that part of England. Is it as lovely as they say, Kelly?" Madison asked.

"Yes, it is," Kelly said.

"Of course, there isn't much to see at Middleborough. All of the most scenic viewpoints are on Willingham." Theodore said coolly.

Everyone at the table looked at Theodore. Kelly felt a ripple of cold foreboding course through her.

His mother swept into the void. "Theodore is teasing, of course..." She said, trying to play off his rude comment. But Kelly could see the harsh lines of his face; in another life, he may have said something like this as a joke; but now he was intentionally trying to provoke her.

"No, truly, mother." He reiterated, his face stone-like.

"I suppose everyone is entitled to their own opinion and preferences," Lord Collins said slowly, his jovial manner from earlier in the evening having transformed into wariness. He didn't dare start an argument on the eve of the long-anticipated wedding, but neither could he accept outright insults from the bitter younger man.

"Let's not kid ourselves, we all know which estate is superior." Theo stared directly at Kelly as he said it.

"Theodore!" His mother exclaimed.

"Really, Mother, I..." He tried to continue, but Kelly stood up abruptly, upsetting her chair with a loud *crack*. He looked like he was about to continue, but instead, he grabbed his glass of wine and stormed out of the room.

Kelly's chest heaved with emotion. "Please excuse me," She said as she quickly went out after Theo.

She followed his heavy footsteps into the hall. She heard him start to mount the stairs, to his private rooms, she assumed. She quickened her step to catch up with him.

"What on Earth did you mean by that?" She said angrily as she reached the foot of the stairs.

He froze, and then slowly turned around to face her. "Why don't you tell me? You seem to have my motivations all figured out now that you know all my secrets." He said coldly.

"Oh no, every time I think I have you figured out, you find some other new way to crush me." She threw back.

"So, you just thought you would go to the source? Ask my mother about my personal business? That's a new low Kelly, even for you." He said.

"Low? What have I ever done to you?" She asked, shocked.

"You came to London to trick me into marrying you."

"I came to London to try and get you to honor a legal contract. A contract that any decent man would have honored years ago. But I was honest with you, which is more than you deserved after the way you ignored me all those years." She said angrily, all the old hurt and fear of insufficiency rising to the surface.

"And I was honest with you. Marriage is a nightmare, and I did my best to tell you that. Even if we start with the best of intentions, it will all go to hell in the end. But you wouldn't be swayed. And now here we are, with no other choice." His eyes were darkening with anger, and his voice was growing louder.

"It's only a nightmare if we let it be, Theo! I know your father was cruel to you and your mother, but I would never do anything to hurt you. I love you!" She exclaimed, tears brimming in her eyes.

"But you did exactly that! You betrayed me, went behind my back, and tried to deceitfully manipulate me with your knowledge. That isn't love."

Kelly felt as if someone had punched her in the stomach. "You are wrong," She said. "But I will not stand by and listen to you insult my family and my home…"

He cut her off: "It doesn't matter; as soon as we are married, it will all be mine anyways." He said nastily.

Her voice shook with anger, "Maybe you are more like your father than anyone thinks, Theodore."

Theo took a step back as if she had struck him. Then he turned on his heel and disappeared up the stairs. As Kelly stared after him, she felt a warm hand on her arm. She turned to see Madison standing behind her.

"Did you hear everything?" Kelly asked morosely.

Madison sighed and put her arms around her friend. "Oh, sweetheart."

Chapter 28

"Tell him we cannot wait any longer. We need to be on our way to the church." Lady Alston said. She had acquired a cane so that she did not exert herself so much while walking, and she tapped it impatiently on the floor as she sent her butler upstairs to retrieve her son.

"That is not necessary. I am ready, Mother," Theo said as he descended the stairway. He took her arm and helped her into the carriage waiting outside, but offered no other comment.

"That scene last night was ghastly, Theo," Eleanor said as soon as the horses jolted the carriage away. He had stayed in his rooms all last night, and she had been so angry she hadn't dared to knock for fear of what she might say to her son. "I know that you were taught better manners than that, so I will not waste my time lecturing you about proper decorum."

Theo cringed. He had embarrassed her, and he felt bad about it. His mother had always been a faithful ally, and she undoubtedly deserved a better performance from him. "I am sorry for how I made you feel, Mother. I did not mean to hurt you."

"Me? Hurt me?" She said sharply. "Have you gone daft?"

He was momentarily taken aback. His mother rarely used a harsh tone. In his whole childhood, he had only heard his mother raise her voice a handful of times. Maybe only once or twice at him.

"Mother, I…"

"Hear me now, Theodore. I have tried your entire life to protect you, and in doing so I have done you a disservice. While I tried to keep you from experiencing pain, I also kept you from experiencing love."

"That is nonsense, Mother. I love you immeasurably." He protested. She smiled slightly but shook her head.

"You never saw a girl on the street and longed to meet her and know her name. You never had an adolescent crush on the older sister of one of your schoolmates. You certainly never had a youthful sweetheart. And because of all of that, when true love came knocking you had no idea what was in front of you." She said sadly.

Theo looked doubtful. "Mother, I think you are overestimating what there is between Kelly and me…"

"I heard Kelly when she told me she loved you weeks ago, and I heard her again last night. Trust me, Theo, no woman would put herself through the trials you have made that girl endure if she did not love you. And she will prove her love again when she shows up at the church and walks down the aisle."

"All that will prove is that she is desperate to protect her family and her home," Theo argued.

"No, it will show that despite everything that has passed between you, she is still not willing to give up on the man she loves." His mother said firmly.

The carriage rocked to a halt, and Theo knew they had arrived. But he didn't move to exit; he sat there in contemplative silence with his mother.

Finally, he spoke. "How do I know that her love won't sour, the way yours did for father? I cannot help that I am like him; eventually, things will deteriorate." He said quietly.

His mother grasped his hands in her own and looked directly into his intense blue eyes, the mirror of her own. "Because I didn't love your father. I wanted things to work out between us, I wanted to create a happy home. But I never loved him." She shook her head again. "And most importantly, he never loved me."

Slowly, Theodore nodded, the motion becoming gradually more confident and resolute. He alighted from the carriage, a new sureness of purpose in his step.

Kelly stood in silence as her mother's maid finished lacing up her gown. Her mother, Claire, stood a few paces away. When the maid finished, she reached for the necklace laid out on the dressing table, but Claire shooed her away. "I can take it from here." She said. "Please go downstairs and see that the carriage is ready; we will be leaving very soon."

The woman bobbed a curtsy and left the room. Kelly's mother fastened the necklace around her daughter's slim neck and then reached up to slightly adjust the fresh flowers that were woven into her hair.

Slowly, she turned Kelly around and pressed her hand to Kelly's cheek.

"I know things are not well between you and Theodore." She said sadly. "I am so sorry for it. I had so hoped…" She paused and sighed. "There was such affection between you two when you were younger. I hoped that it would grow into something more, something that would make a happy marriage between you."

"Oh, Mama," Kelly could see the tears in her mother's eyes, and she struggled to keep her own at bay. "For me, it did." She said softly. "But for Theo…it just isn't that simple."

"I feel like I am taking you to a prison, on what should be the happiest day of your life." The guilt rang in her voice.

But Kelly shook her head. "No, please, do not do that to yourself. I have always known I would marry Theo. It is true, the circumstances are not what I thought they would be. But…I love him. So, I will do as I have promised, to you and him." She took her mother's hand and kissed it tenderly.

The older woman nodded, her smile still sad. "Well, we had best be going if we are to arrive on time." Together they made their way downstairs into the entry hall, where Kelly's father was waiting for them.

"Ah, both of my ladies look so beautiful," He said with a smile, kissing each of their cheeks. "I believe the carriage is waiting for us?" He looked over at the housekeeper and butler, standing against the wall. They nodded affirmatively.

The butler came forward and opened the door, and Lord Collins escorted Kelly's mother down the stairs. Kelly followed behind them.

"Ho there! Don't you make a stunnn...stunning bride," said a loud voice, familiar but slurred. Kelly was astounded to see Christopher, Lord Bowden, making his way down the street. He stopped and leaned upon the edge of the Collins' carriage, taking in the wedding-attired family. "Too...too bad you're wasting yourself on a cold fish like Alston." He said, stumbling a little over his words.

Kelly looked at him strangely. "Lord Bowden, are you drunk?" She asked with consternation.

He laughed rudely. "Foxed, I believe is the term."

"Sir, we really must be on our way," Kelly's father interceded. He had never met Christopher Bowden, but he certainly didn't like the impression he was getting now.

"Rrrright," Lord Bowden slurred, pointing his finger around wildly, before settling on a direction. "To the church."

"Yes, excuse us," Lord Collins said, trying to signal an end to the conversation by moving his wife forward towards the carriage.

"Ha," The young lord snorted. "He won't be there, you know."

"Pardon me?" Kelly's eyes widened.

Her father sighed. "Kelly, ignore this man, get on up into the carriage."

"One moment, father," Kelly said. She turned back to Lord Bowden. "What do you mean, 'he won't be there'?"

"Alston isn't going to show," Bowden said, giving her a pitying look. "It's making the rounds in all the gentleman's clubs. He doesn't want to be married, and he won't be forced by some country girl."

Kelly closed her eyes and bit her lip as pain coursed through her.

Now Kelly's mother interceded. "Are you saying Lord Alston means to stand my daughter up publicly, today?" She demanded, her eyes widening with concern.

Lord Bowden shrugged, an action which off-balanced him. He had to grab the rail of the carriage again for support to keep from stumbling over. "Looks like it," He said.

"We must send someone over to the Alston townhouse at once, we need to know…" Kelly's mother began, but Kelly interrupted her.

"No, Mother. I do know." Kelly said, her voice tortured with pain. "I should have known all along."

"Kelly…" Her mother tried to say something, but there was nothing she could think of. Her heart broke for her daughter as she took her in her arms.

Kelly didn't attempt to stop the tears from falling as she buried her face in her mother's shoulder. After a few moments, she looked up at her father, who stood by helplessly. "Father, can we go home, please? I cannot stand to be in London a moment longer."

He nodded, "Yes, of course. We can leave immediately." He said, and then guided his wife and daughter inside so he could make the arrangements.

Chapter 29

From where he stood at the back of the church, Theo gazed at the small assembly of guests seated to witness the ceremony: his mother, a great aunt who lived nearby, a neighbor who lived near the Alston and Collins families, a few of Kelly's relatives. By custom, the ceremony itself was small, while the wedding breakfast that followed would be well-attended and elaborate.

But it didn't appear that there would be a wedding breakfast. He heard footsteps approaching behind him. "What time is it?" He asked.

"It's a quarter past eleven," Henry answered. "The pastor says that if Kelly does not arrive soon, there will not be enough time to complete the ceremony before noon, and it will have to be postponed…"

When Theo didn't respond, Henry continued. "The Collins' house isn't far, I can go and see what is delaying them. Maybe someone has fallen ill and they have been too caught up to send word." Henry offered.

"No," Repeated Theo. "I need to go myself."

It's my fault, it's my fault. The words coursed through Theo's head over and over as he rode the short distance from the church to the Collins' residence. He shouldn't have provoked her so cruelly the night before. It was more than any person should have to endure, as his mother had so wisely pointed out. Of course, she was questioning whether she wanted to go through with the wedding.

Or maybe she didn't love him after all. The thought crept into his head unbidden. *Maybe his mother was wrong. No,* he dismissed the thought firmly. He would go to her now and apologize. He would say that he was willing to give their marriage a try, to try and see what happiness they could build together. It wasn't a declaration of love, but it was as much as he had to give. Surely it would be enough for Kelly.

As he approached the Collins' townhouse, he could see some hustle and bustle outside. It appeared that heavy trunks were being loaded into a wagon. The Collins' butler was standing at the wagon directing the young male servants, while the housekeeper stood at the open door to the residence issuing orders to maids and valets.

"Lord Alston," The butler stepped back in surprise when he saw Theodore dismounting.

"Please inform Miss Collins that I am here and need to speak to her immediately," Theo said.

"I am afraid that I cannot do that, Lord Alston," The butler said, his nerves apparent. Theo sighed. Kelly must have forbidden the staff to allow him access to her.

"Look, I must speak to Miss Collins. I have wronged her, but I need the chance to explain myself so we can get things back on schedule." It was hard for him to admit out loud, especially to a servant, but he would do whatever was necessary to speak to Kelly.

"Yes, sir, I'm sure...." The older man sighed with resignation. "However, Miss Collins is not here."

"She's not here? Did she leave for the church?" Theo glanced behind him; he couldn't have missed her on the road, could he?

"No, my lord. Miss Collins and her parents...have returned to Middleborough Manor."

"Middleborough Manor?" Theo repeated, his mind suddenly going blank.

"Yes, my lord. They have left London...permanently. The staff is to close up the house and follow with all due haste."

"I see," Theo said, his eyes and tone darkening. *Kelly was gone. And she was not coming back.*

"They are almost out of time," Madison said worriedly. "I should have gone myself...I could have brought her around, I am sure."

"Theo wanted to go himself," Henry said.

Madison snorted in a most undignified way. "Yes, Theo has such a stunning record for handling these sorts of delicate situations." She said sarcastically.

"Fair enough," Henry conceded. "But really, don't you think it's time that we stayed out of it? You cannot continue to meddle after they are married, Maddy."

"Let's see them married and then we can argue the particulars," Madison crossed her arms and walked to the doors of the church, open to let the bright sunshine pour in. "Henry! He's back!" She called as she spotted Theo riding up.

Henry rushed out to meet him. "Is Miss Collins coming behind you? Shall I tell the pastor that we will be proceeding momentarily?" He asked hopefully.

"No," Theo said stonily. "Tell everyone to go home. She's not coming."

Chapter 30

*H*enry observed his friend from the doorway before he made himself known. Theo was seated in a heavy leather chair, facing the window. Their gentleman's club was bustling with activity as usual, but Theo had chosen a secluded corner of a quiet room. Henry had almost missed Theo entirely as he had walked the rooms searching for him. Clearly, Theo wanted to be alone and undisturbed. So naturally, Henry poured himself and Theo a finger of brandy and pulled up a chair adjacent to him.

Theo glanced up at Henry as he handed him the glass, but took it without speaking. It had been almost a week since his aborted wedding. He had spent most of those days just like this; brooding darkly. Occasionally, he took out his horse and galloped until they were both breathless.

They didn't talk but sat in silence born of long friendship. As they sat there, a few more men entered the room, taking up cues to play at the billiards table behind them that had been previously unoccupied. Theodore tried to ignore them.

"It's a shame, really. She was a good-looking girl." The first said.

"Yes; not the kind you notice right away. Brunettes aren't really in fashion, you know. But once you looked at her, she was very fair," Agreed the second.

A third chuckled. "Well, I certainly noticed, for all the good that it did me."

One of the others clapped him on the shoulder. "Don't take it personally, chap. She didn't even seem to consider anyone else."

"I didn't understand that. What made her so determined? There were plenty of other gentlemen who were interested."

"Family obligations and all that, I suppose." One of the men said as he leaned over and took a shot at the table.

"Did you hear that Alston was going to stand her up? My valet had it from someone in his household that they had a terrible row the night before, and that there was no way Alston was going to go through with it."

Theo and Henry sat up instantly.

"Sure did, I told her myself," Christopher Bowden said smugly as he lined up to take the next shot. "Granted, I was still a bit foxed from the night before, but I think I got the point across."

"What did you say?" Theodore growled as he ripped the billiards cue out of the other man's hands.

Lord Bowden stumbled backward a few steps in shock. The other two gentlemen's surprise showed on their faces. "Alston, we had no idea you were in here…" One of them started to say, but Theodore's menacing look cut him off.

"What did you say about talking to Kelly?" Theo said fiercely, advancing on Christopher.

"I, um…I spoke to her on the morning of the wedding." He admitted, looking nervous. He glanced at his two friends for support, but they were clearly not going to get in Theo's way. He looked murderous.

"You spoke to her? And what did you say?"

"I only repeated what I had been hearing all night," Christopher said defensively.

"And what was that? That I wasn't going to be at the wedding? That I was going to stand her up?" Theo was nearly yelling. Henry stepped in, putting his hand on Theodore's shoulder.

"Theo, take a breath, man," He said, but Theo shook his hand off.

"Tell me now, what did you say to her, or…" Theo let his eyes finish the threat.

"Alright! I told her that you weren't going to show up at the church. That you wouldn't be forced into marriage by some nobody country girl. But I'm telling you, I was only repeating what I had heard…" He didn't get a chance to finish, because Theodore punched him in the gut. He staggered backward, and Henry intervened, catching Theo's arm before he could land another hit.

Theo was vibrating with rage; Henry knew that if Theo was determined, he wouldn't be able to restrain him for long. "Get him out of here, now," Henry advised the other two men, nodding at Lord Bowden. They did as he suggested, each grabbing their friend under an arm and leading him out of the room. When they were out of sight, Henry counted to ten and then released his hold on Theodore.

Theo stalked away from him, to the window. His face was unreadable. After a few moments, he reached over and downed the brandy that Henry had poured for him earlier. Without a word, Henry went to the sideboard and refilled the heavy crystal glass.

"What are you going to do?" He asked as he handed it back to Theo.

Theo stared at the amber liquid for a long time. Then he brought it to his lips and drank it down steadily. "I am going to go and get my fiancée." He said. "You'd better pour me one more; I'm going to need all the liquid courage I can to get me through this."

Henry gave a small chuckle and indulged his friend.

Chapter 31

Kelly spread out a blanket on the bank of the stream. Her mother had sent her with a basket of food; it was brimming with rolls, hunks of cheese, fresh fruit, even some sweet pastries. Why was it that people always tried to feed you when you were grieving? Kelly wondered to herself. She ate from the basket absentmindedly, not really tasting the delicacies her mother had so lovingly arranged. Nothing seemed to have flavor anymore. She supposed that was what happened when your heart was broken.

Her mother and father, bless them, had been nothing but kind and loving. There had been no words about what the breakdown of her engagement meant for their estate or their family. But Kelly knew eventually it was a conversation that would have to be had. She sighed wistfully; she had done everything she could.

She was trying to let go, trying to let her beloved Middleborough soothe her soul. In the moment, when she had learned of his desertion, she could think of nothing else except getting out of London. London had been where her love for him and grown and taken shape; where she had seen the warm and humorous side of him, where he had kissed her and awoken parts of her body she hadn't known existed, where they had made love.

Kelly wanted to regret giving herself to him, knew that was the proper thing to do. Any good young woman would have been embarrassed and woebegone at the loss of her virtue to a man who would not become her husband. But Kelly would hold on to those precious moments forever. He hadn't been able to love her with his soul, but at least he had loved her with his body. She wanted to cherish the memory.

But, oh, how she hurt. Sometimes just the beating of her heart itself felt painful. Her home, secluded in the country, was supposed to be a balm to her wounded heart. But here, too, memories of him abounded. How far would she have to go to escape him? She wondered sadly.

She was so caught up in her thoughts, that she did not hear him approaching. It was his voice that startled her out of her musing.

"May I sit with you?" Theo asked.

Kelly felt a shiver go up her spine at the sound of his voice. She pressed her eyes closed, trying to hold at bay the rush of emotions, trying to summon all of her inner strength. "It might be better if you don't." She managed to say.

"I deserve that," Theo said, sitting down next to her anyway.

She told herself not to look at him, sure that if she did she would go to pieces. "What are you doing here, Theodore?"

He didn't answer immediately. Instead, he said: "You are still wearing my mother's ring." There was a note of surprise and...was it pleasure?...in his voice.

Hastily Kelly pulled it off of her hand and dropped it onto the blanket next to him as if it were burning her finger. She had intended to send it back to Lady Alston, of course, but hadn't been able to bring herself to do it.

Theo picked the ring up and turned it around between his fingers. Then it disappeared into his closed palm. Kelly let out a little sigh of relief; at least that was done now.

"I owe you an explanation, Kelly, and..." He began to say, turning to look at her. But when she met his eyes, he lost all coherent thought. The pain, longing, and love were too much for him to bear. Leaning forward, he cupped the back of her head in his hand and kissed her tenderly.

She broke away, "Theo, I cannot do this again," She said, her voice fraught with emotion.

"Kelly," He whispered, keeping his hand tangled in her hair and touching his forehead to hers. "I am so sorry." He waited for her to say something, but when she didn't he kept talking for fear that she would pull away and not hear another word from him. "I was never going to leave you. I was waiting at the church. I could hardly believe it when I went to your house and the staff informed me you had left."

"But," Kelly pulled back slightly, but she braced herself against Theo's arm and then didn't let go. "Lord Bowden said...he..he...he said that you weren't coming. That you would never allow yourself to be coerced into marrying me." Tears started to fall down her cheeks, and her voice trembled.

"He was wrong, Kelly. I don't know who he heard it from or how the rumor got started. But I was there. I was waiting there for you." He said ardently. Kelly let out a little sob.

"But you didn't...you didn't want to marry me." She said, biting her lower lip to keep it from wavering visibly.

Theo shook his head, pulling her back close to him. "Can you forgive me, Kelly, for being so blind?" She looked confused as he smiled at her. "I want to marry you more than anything in the world. I love you." He whispered.

"Oh, Theo," She cried, and then she closed the few inches between them and pressed her lips to his. She kissed him with all the love and emotion that had been boiling inside of her for months, maybe even years.

He trailed kisses across her forehead, cheek, neck, and shoulder. When they finally came up for air, he held out his hand between them and opened it to reveal the glowing amber-colored topaz stone. "I was too afraid to ask you properly before. And, I am still afraid. But I love you, Kelly, and if you will have me, I want to take a chance that we really can have the kind of life and marriage you envision." He breathed out heavily through pursed lips. "Will you marry me?"

Kelly gave a small laugh, and then smiled radiantly as she said, "Yes, Theodore I want nothing more." He slid the ring back onto her finger, and Kelly felt more joy than she had wearing it at any previous moment.

After many long minutes spent holding each other and renewing their love with kisses and touches, Theo drew Kelly to her feet. "I suppose we should head back to the manor. Your mother and father were quite upset that I wouldn't give them any explanation before running off to find you. I imagine your father is ready to challenge me to a duel by this point."

"Papa would never," Kelly reassured him as she gathered up the things she had brought with her. She put her arm through Theo's and allowed him to lead her along the stream, back across the fields and hills where they had shared so many memories. "I was right, you know, when I said that all of this would one day be mine," She teased, motioning to the stream that was the demarcation between their estates.

Theo smiled and pulled her close, wrapping his arms around her. "Well then," He said, "I suppose I was wrong about everything." But when he leaned down and kissed her, he had never felt so right.

Epilogue

Christopher stumbled into the dark room without bothering to try and find the lamp or light a candle. He knew where the decanter was, and that was all that mattered to him at this moment. He gripped his side, which had been wrapped in several layers of sturdy bandages to stabilize and protect from further injury. Right that moment, it didn't feel like it was doing a thing to ease the pain of the rib that Theodore Alston had broken. Hence, he sought the decanter and the fiery liquid within.

He made his way around the low table and the corner of the sofa and reached his goal. Letting out a sigh of relief, he pulled out the stopper and started to pour.

"Ruining a wedding really is bad form, even for you." A voice said disdainfully from behind him. The whiskey sloshed all over the place, and Christopher jumped in surprise. The action caused pain to tear through his side and he swore virulently.

He ignored the voice and poured his drink, more successfully this time. Limping slightly, he turned around and eased himself onto the sofa. "Still have a knack for sneaking in where you don't belong, I see?" He said to the figure seated across from him.

"I don't even have to sneak, Christopher. Your butler admitted me willingly. It is amazing what one can achieve with a little civility." The implication in the comment was harsh.

"Civility is overrated," He took a long drink.

"It is apparent that you think so, based on the way you have been behaving. I have never been ashamed to claim friendship with someone until today."

"Well, then spare yourself the embarrassment and don't claim me as anything," Christopher said spitefully.

"Oh, that it was that simple. But for once, I need something from you."

"What could you possibly need from me that your uppity lord whatever cannot provide?" He scoffed.

"Do not speak of my husband that way." She warned.

"Sorry," Christopher muttered into his glass, but she ignored him and continued.

"I cannot travel for the next several months, and given my condition, I need Henry to stay close to home." She said.

"Your condition?" Christopher sat up and leaned closer, trying to get a better look at her in the dim light filtering in from the street outside.

"I am with child," She said, but waved her hand dismissively as if it was nothing. "But this is not about me."

"Then what is it about?" He asked, his interest piqued despite his disaffection. He winced as he leaned forward and unintentionally aggravated his injury.

"It's about Meera. She has disappeared." Madison said. "And I need you to find her."

If you enjoyed *Meant to be Mine*…

Please leave a positive review on Amazon or Goodreads

Reviews are essential for independent authors! As an emerging author, I read every review you write and take it to heart as I dream up new romances. Your review really does make an impact. It helps other readers find and enjoy these characters and their stories. Thank you for your time. -Cara

Read the rest of the Hesitant Husbands Series:

Love Once Lost

A Love Match for the Marquess

Visit caramaxwellromance.com for previews of upcoming books and special offers. Follow @caramaxwellromance on Instagram for updates and exclusive content.

About the Author

Bringing fresh perspective and punch to the genre readers already know and love, Cara Maxwell is dedicated to writing spirited heroines and irresistible rogues who you will root for every time. A lifetime reader of romance, Cara put pen to paper (or rather, fingers to keyboard) in 2019 and published her first book. She hasn't slowed down from there.

Cara is an avid traveler. As she explores new places, she imagines her characters walking hand-in-hand down a cobblestone path or sharing a passionate kiss in a secluded alcove. Cara is living out her own happily ever after in Seattle, Washington, where she resides with her husband, daughter, and two cats, RoseArt and Etch-a-Sketch.